Welcome to Suite 4B!

Gone to the stables

Shh!! Studying—
please do not disturb!

Mary Beth

<u>GO AWAY!!!</u>

Andie

Hey, guys!
Meet me downstairs in the
common room. Bring popcorn!

Lauren

D0826663

Join Andie, Jina, Mary Beth, and Lauren
for more fun at the Riding Academy!

And coming soon:

Magic's doing great in the big ring, Andie told herself. *Jumping him will be no big deal.* Besides, this might be her last chance to prove to her dad that Magic was the right horse for her. She just had to impress him.

"Let's do it, guy," Andie told the Thoroughbred. She trotted him in a circle, then steered him down the middle of the ring.

As they approached the cavalletti, Magic's ears flicked back and forth. Then his stride quickened, and Andie grabbed a hunk of his mane.

You've jumped a zillion times, she told herself. *This isn't any different.* But it *was* different. She'd never jumped Magic before.

A stride before the fence, Magic arched his neck and leaped into the air...

ANDIE
SHOWS OFF

by Alison Hart

BULLSEYE BOOKS

Random House 🏠 New York

A BULLSEYE BOOK PUBLISHED BY RANDOM HOUSE, INC.

Copyright © 1994 by Random House, Inc., and Alice Leonhardt.
Cover design by Fabia Wargin Design and Creative Media
Applications, Inc. Cover art copyright © 1994 by Dan Burr.
All rights reserved under International and Pan-American Copyright
Conventions. Published in the United States by Random House, Inc.,
New York, and simultaneously in Canada by Random House of
Canada Limited, Toronto.

Library of Congress Catalog Card Number: 94-67691

ISBN: 0-679-85697-8

RL: 4.9

Manufactured in the United States of America

10 9 8 7 6 5 4 3 2

RIDING ACADEMY is a trademark of Random House, Inc

"I love Halloween," Andie Perez said as she munched on a bite-sized Snickers. She was sitting cross-legged on her bed in suite 4B. A bowl of candy was balanced on her knees. "All these yummy things to eat."

"Hey! Those are for the kids!" Mary Beth Finney, one of her roommates, protested. Swooping down on Andie, Mary Beth grabbed the bowl. Andie held it tight.

"You're eating all the good candy," Mary Beth said, yanking hard on the bowl.

"No way." Andie yanked right back. "We bought plenty of stuff for the trick-or-treaters."

"Would you two stop?" Lauren Remick said. Hands on her hips, she looked at her roommates disgustedly. Andie grinned back at her.

She loved making Mary Beth and Lauren mad.

Jina Williams, their fourth roommate, lay on her bed reading, pretending to ignore the others. It was Sunday night. Foxhall Academy, the private boarding school the girls attended, had just finished up a busy weekend of Halloween activities with Manchester Academy, a private boys' school.

Tonight was officially Halloween, and the staff members' children would be going around to the different dorms for trick-or-treating. Earlier in the week, Andie, Jina, Mary Beth, and Lauren had pitched in and bought several bags of candy to pass out to the kids.

"On second thought, maybe I will give the bowl to you, Finney," Andie said, suddenly letting go. Mary Beth flew backward, landing hard on the floor. Candy bars flew everywhere.

Andie burst out laughing.

"You creep," Mary Beth fumed, her freckled cheeks reddening. Just then, someone knocked on the door, and several little voices yelled, "Trick or treat!"

"Quick, they're here!" Lauren dropped down on her knees to help Mary Beth pick up the spilled candy. Her blond braid fell over her shoulder.

Andie jumped off the bed and strode to the door. The suite was so small she had to step over Mary Beth, who was frantically dumping candy back in the bowl.

"Really, Andie," Lauren grumbled, "the least you can do is help."

"I am. I'm answering the door," Andie said. Jina jumped off the bed, and the two of them reached the door at the same time. When Andie opened it, three kids about six years old smiled up at them.

"Oh, aren't they cute," Jina said, her golden eyes lighting up. Putting her palms on her knees, she bent over so she was their height.

"Let's see. You must be an angel," she said to a little girl with wings. "You're a cowboy," she said to a red-haired boy with a holster and gun. "And *you* must be a—"

Straightening up, Jina tapped her cheek with her finger and pretended to think as she studied the little girl who wore a fuzzy headdress and tail.

Andie shook her head. She had never seen Jina act so goofy. Usually her roommate was quiet and serious.

3

"A wion," the little girl answered, smiling.

"What's a wion?" Andie whispered to Lauren.

"A lion, dodo," Lauren promptly replied. She was peering over Andie's shoulder. Mary Beth had squeezed in next to Jina.

"Aren't you guys adorable!" Mary Beth squealed as she held out the bowl of candy.

Adorable? Andie grimaced. The lion had chocolate smeared on her face, the cowboy had gum on his lips, and the angel's tutu was dotted with gross, sticky stuff.

Andie wrinkled her nose as three sets of grubby fingers dove into the bowl and greedily scooped out candy. "Hey, save some for the other kids," she said. Grabbing the bowl from Mary Beth, she held it out of reach.

The cowboy pulled out his gun and pointed it at Andie. "We want more candy," he growled, "or else."

Andie frowned and bent over. "Or else what?" she asked in a low voice.

"Uh-h-h." The cowboy's eyes widened, and he lowered his gun.

"Since I'm the sheriff of this suite," Andie said, "I suggest you get on your horse and ride out of here. Or I might have to steal *your* bag of treats."

The cowboy gulped and quickly slipped his gun back into the holster. "Let's go to the next room," he said to the lion and the angel.

"You didn't have to scare him to death, Andie," Lauren said when the kids had scurried away.

Mary Beth let out a loud sigh. "They were so-o-o-o cute. They reminded me of my little brothers and sister. Last year, Benji was a vampire. We used lipstick for blood and bought him these big wax fangs. And we covered boxes with foil to make a robot costume for Reed. And Tammy—"

"Will you shut up, Finney?" Andie cut in. She didn't want to hear about Mary Beth's family. In six days it would be Parents' Weekend and her father was coming. That was all she cared about.

Ignoring Andie, Mary Beth dropped onto her quilt-covered bed. "Tammy wore an adorable bunny outfit with floppy ears. And we even dressed up Dogums."

Andie rolled her eyes. *Dressing a dog? How lame.*

Still holding the candy bowl, Andie flopped down onto Jina's bed, which was next to the door. Jina was leaning against the doorjamb, looking out for more trick-and-treaters.

"Just think, last year I was trick-or-treating with all my friends at home," Lauren said. She sighed as she sat down next to Mary Beth. "I was a cat and my best friend was a mouse."

"How juvenile," Andie muttered. As she unwrapped a lollipop, she tried to remember what she'd done last Halloween. It was around the time she'd been kicked out of her last boarding school. Her father had grounded her and she'd been stuck in her room all night.

"So what were *you* doing last Halloween, Jina?" Lauren asked.

"Oh, my mom hosted some big charity bash," Jina said, still gazing into the hall. Jina's mom was a big-shot talk show host. "It was really boring."

Abruptly, she straightened and waved to Andie. "Here come some more kids. Bring the bowl over. Oh, these guys are really cute."

Squealing in unison, Lauren and Mary Beth jumped off the bed and raced to the doorway. Slowly, Andie followed. She tried to remember the last time she'd been trick-or-treating. It must have been in fourth grade, before her parents split up.

"Oo-oo-oooh, look at you," Lauren was saying. Andie peered over her shoulder. A tiny girl dressed like a princess stood next to her taller brother, who was dressed like a pirate. Mr. Vassaloti, one of the upper-grade math teachers, stood at the end of the hall, beaming proudly.

The two kids took some candy, then moved on to the next suite. Jina, Lauren, and Mary Beth waved after them. Mary Beth sniffed quietly.

Andie pulled the lollipop out of her mouth. "Are you still thinking about your dopey brothers and sister, Finney? I mean, you're going to see them this weekend."

Mary Beth brightened. "That's right." Turning, she came back into the room. "My whole family's staying over Friday and Saturday night. They even found a motel that allowed pets, so they're bringing Dogums."

"My mom and dad are coming, too," Lauren said. She walked over to her dresser and pulled her nightshirt from the drawer. "Is your mom coming, Jina?"

"I think so," Jina said, her voice flat. Arms

crossed, she continued to stare into the hall. Andie wondered if Jina was worried that her mom wouldn't make it to Parents' Weekend. Jina's mom, Myra Golden, was even busier than Andie's dad. Myra had her own talk show, *Myra Golden Live*.

Andie brushed a pile of candy wrappers off her own bed and fell backward onto it. Her dark hair flew around her shoulders and several strands got stuck on her lollipop.

"Well, *my* dad's coming," she announced loudly, "for the whole weekend. And I'm going to ride Magic for him."

Jina turned away from the hall. "But you haven't even been allowed on Magic yet."

"I know. But tomorrow's the big day." Andie ripped her hair off the lollipop. "Caufield says he's ready."

"Wow." Mary Beth's eyes were wide. "Aren't you afraid he'll buck you off?"

Andie snorted. Only Mary Beth would ask a stupid question like that. Even after two months in the Foxhall riding program, she was still half scared of horses.

"No way. I've been grooming him every day, and longing him so he obeys my voice commands," Andie explained. "He trusts me now.

And he's not shying at everything since he had his eye operation."

"That's great," Lauren said. Grabbing her shower bucket, she headed into the bathroom that the four girls shared. "Call me if any more kids show up."

"That's neat your dad will get to see you ride him," Jina said.

Andie sat up and set the lollipop on her desk. "Yeah. I'm going to show him how much Magic has changed. The semester is almost over, and I kept my part of the deal—my grades are pretty decent. Now my dad needs to keep *his* part of the deal and buy Magic."

"I hope Magic does okay when your dad comes," Mary Beth said, her voice doubtful. "He was pretty crazy."

"He was *never* crazy," Andie said sharply. "He just couldn't see out of one eye. This weekend he's going to do great," she added. "You just wait, Finney."

Mary Beth shrugged. "Okay. It's just that a week isn't a very long time."

Andie flopped over, turning her back on her roommates. *It's long enough*, she thought. But her stomach was tightening into a knot.

9

What if her father came and Magic *did* act up?

The beautiful Thoroughbred had been doing so well. Still, Andie had no idea how he would behave when she finally mounted him. Mary Beth was right. Magic *had* been crazy.

Then another fear hit her. What if her father didn't show up for Parents' Weekend?

She knew how busy he was at work. But the last time he'd called, he'd *promised* he'd come.

Andie buried her head in her pillow. Her father had broken promises before.

But this time he won't, Andie told herself, punching the pillow fiercely. *This time he'll come and Magic will be perfect and Dad will agree that he should be my horse.*

He just *had* to or she'd *die.*

2

"Walk on," Andie said, her voice crisp. In front of her, on the end of the longe line, Magic moved from the halt to the walk. His stride was long and energetic as he circled Andie. His dark-mahogany coat gleamed, and the white star between his eyes glistened from hours of grooming.

"Trot," Andie commanded. Magic whisked his tail and broke into an easy trot. A brisk November wind whistled through the trees, swirling the leaves that had fallen into the paddock behind the new barn.

Magic snorted and tossed his head, but Andie just grinned. Two weeks ago, it would have been a snort of fear. This time Magic was felling good.

Playfully, he trotted around Andie, his

movements light and athletic. Though Andie held a longe whip in her right hand, she didn't have to use it to encourage him to stay out on the circle.

Today Andie was going to ride Magic. She couldn't wait. He was already saddled and bridled. Andie had secured the stirrups by pulling the leathers through the stirrup irons so they wouldn't flap while she longed him. Then she'd twisted the reins and tucked them under the throatlatch so they couldn't get loose.

"He looks nice and relaxed," Mrs. Caufield called. Foxhall's riding program director came up to the fence and leaned on the top rail. She wore a goose down vest over her sweater. A paisley scarf hid her graying brown hair. "You've learned a lot since you first started longing him."

Andie hid a smile. Mrs. Caufield had made longing look so easy. When Andie had tried it, she quickly found out it wasn't. Magic had bolted and broken away, pulling the longe line right through her fingers.

"Whoa," Andie called. Magic stopped dead. Turning, he looked at her, his ears pricked eagerly.

"Good boy," Andie said, dropping the whip

on the ground. Then, gathering up the longe line, she slowly walked toward him. When she got close enough, he stuck out his nose and snuffled her fingers.

Andie patted his neck. "No treat today," she whispered in his ear. "Caufield's watching."

"Are you ready to ride him?" Mrs. Caufield asked as she opened the gate and walked into the paddock.

Andie nodded, her heart racing with excitement. With trembling fingers, she unsnapped the longe line, which was hooked to the outside of the snaffle bit.

Mrs. Caufield pulled the line over Magic's poll and through the bit on the inside.

She eyed Andie. "Nervous?"

Andie shook her head vigorously. "No way! I've been waiting for this forever."

"You haven't been just waiting," Mrs. Caufield reminded her. "You've been learning more about Magic and teaching him to trust you."

"I know." Andie let down the stirrups on both sides and glanced around, half expecting to see her roommates. But the area behind the new barn was quiet. The school horses were kept in the larger barn farther down the drive, so most of the girls in the riding program hung around there.

Mrs. Caufield stepped back and gazed at Magic. "He's a different horse since he first came to Foxhall," she said, patting him on the neck.

Magic nudged Andie with his nose, as if to ask her what was going on.

"Much calmer," Mrs. Caufield went on. "Still, he'll probably tense up when you get on him. Remember, he's had some bad experiences with other riders."

"Right." Andie frowned. Magic's previous trainer had used spurs and a whip to force the scared Thoroughbred over jumps.

"We need to establish a calming routine for him," the director continued. "What do you usually do when he sees something scary on his walks?"

"Umm..." Andie racked her brains. "Circle him away from whatever it is, then gradually bring him back to it. That's what one book I read suggested. It seems to work."

"Good." Mrs. Caufield crossed her arms. "Today, when you feel him getting nervous, don't pull on the reins. Circle him until he's settled, then move him forward again. Now put your longing stuff away and get your riding helmet."

Andie handed Mrs. Caufield the reins, then picked up the longe whip. She walked toward the gate, winding up the longe line.

I'm not scared, she told herself.

She pulled her hair back into a ponytail, stuck her helmet onto her head, and snapped the chin strap. Then, taking a deep breath, she turned and faced Magic. Ears forward, he watched her with big, curious eyes.

He really is different now, Andie thought. *He knows I'd never do anything to hurt him.*

When she reached the Thoroughbred, she stroked his neck once, then took the reins from Mrs. Caufield.

"Let me give you a leg up," the director said, putting both hands under Andie's knee.

"One, two, *three*," Mrs. Caufield said, lifting her up. Andie swung her right leg over the cantle and settled into the saddle.

When she looked down, she gasped. She couldn't help it. She'd been on Magic only once, and she didn't remember his being so tall.

Mrs. Caufield laughed. "He's not any bigger than Ranger," she said, reminding Andie of the school horse that Andie often rode.

"I—I know," Andie stammered. She wanted to kick herself. She was never scared of anything. What was she so worried about now?

Immediately, she thought of the day Magic had first arrived at Foxhall. He'd bolted off with Katherine Parks, the school's dressage instructor. Then the Thoroughbred had reared, throwing Katherine off. And she was one of the best riders Andie knew.

Mrs. Caufield reached up and grasped the calf of Andie's black boot. "Hey. If I didn't think this was okay, I'd never let you get on him," she said.

Andie forced a smile. "I know. It's just that—"

She wasn't sure what her problem was. Maybe it was that her father was coming to see her ride him on Saturday. Maybe it was that she wanted to own Magic so much. Maybe it was that she'd waited so long for this day.

Or maybe it was all those things.

Andie took a deep breath. Magic hadn't moved a muscle. He was bobbing his head and chewing on his bit as if he were bored.

"Relax your legs against his sides, but don't

use leg aids," Mrs. Caufield instructed. "That way he won't worry that you're going to use spurs. Instead, give the voice commands you used for longing. We'll gradually add leg aids later."

Andie nodded, then gathered her reins until she had light contact. "Walk," she told Magic, using the same tone of voice she used for longing.

Magic instantly strode forward. Andie took a few deep breaths, trying to stay calm. She didn't want Magic to know how nervous she was.

"Just circle around me at a walk," Mrs. Caufield called. "Stay alert, sit deep, and don't tense up."

Don't tense up, Andie repeated silently, willing her body to relax. Magic moved easily and smoothly. Andie started to grin. It was like riding a cloud!

"Circle and change directions, then halt," the riding director called.

Andie closed her left fingers on the rein and Magic immediately turned to the inside. When they reached the opposite rail, she asked him to halt with a firm *whoa*. He stopped in his tracks.

Andie felt a rush of relief. Reaching down, she patted Magic on his silky neck. He was really listening to her.

Mrs. Caufield grinned at them. "He's doing great. Keep practicing walking and halts for about ten more minutes. Then we'll quit."

"Okay." Andie urged Magic forward. Suddenly, his head went up and his ears flicked back and forth.

Jina was leading Superstar around the side of the new barn. The gray horse wore a bright blue blanket. When Superstar caught sight of Magic, he let out an ear-splitting whinny.

Jina looked up and saw Andie and Magic. Immediately she spun Superstar around and led him back to the barn. But it was too late.

Andie felt Magic tense as he stared at the departing horse. After nickering a reply, he bagan to prance nervously.

Andie tightened her hold on the reins. Magic tossed his head, then swung his haunches sideways. His left flank hit the rail with a *crack*.

Mrs. Caufield hollered something, but Andie couldn't hear her very well. Tugging hard on the reins, she dug her left heel into

Magic's side, trying to move him away from the rail.

Startled, the Thoroughbred jumped in the air. Andie grabbed his mane and held tight. Keeping her weight in her heels, she tried to sit deep.

"Whoa!" Mrs. Caufield called in a firm voice. "Tell him to whoa."

"Whoa," Andie repeated loudly. Magic stopped dead. She could feel him trembling beneath her.

Andie bit her lip, forcing back tears. She couldn't believe that Magic had almost crashed through the fence. Even after the operation on his eye and all the time she'd spent with him, nothing had changed. Mary Beth was right.

Magic was still crazy!

"Andie!" Mrs. Caufield said sharply. Frowning, she strode across the ring. "What was *that* all about?"

"Magic went nuts," Andie said, trying to keep the disappointment out of her voice.

Mrs. Caufield grabbed the inside rein and put her hand on Magic's neck. "No, Andie. *Magic* did not go nuts. *You* were the one who caused the problem."

Startled, Andie looked down at the riding director. Mrs. Caufield was still frowning at her.

"*Me?*" Andie protested. She should have known Caufield would blame her. Grown-ups were always doing that.

"Yes. You did everything I told you *not* to do."

Andie opened her mouth to protest again, but the riding director raised a hand to silence her. "Think before you say anything. Then tell me what *you* did when Magic saw Superstar."

Slowly, Andie shut her mouth. She felt herself flush as she realized Mrs. Caufield was right. Magic had reacted to Superstar like any young horse who was full of himself. *She* was the one who had done everything wrong.

Embarrassed, Andie dropped her gaze to Magic's neck. "I tensed up, pulled on the reins, and kicked him," she admitted finally.

Mrs. Caufield nodded. "That's right. Now what *should* you have done?"

"Circled him until he settled and—" Andie looked hesitantly at Mrs. Caufield "—used voice commands."

Mrs. Caufield gave another nod. "That's right. He stopped dead when you said 'whoa.'"

Andie bit her lip. She felt terrible. Her first time officially riding Magic and she'd acted like a beginner.

"So, who has lots to learn here?" Mrs. Caufield asked.

"Me," Andie croaked.

"No, both of you." Mrs. Caufield rapped on Andie's boot. "Magic is a special horse. He's going to be more sensitive than any horse you've ever ridden. You're a good rider, Andie, but you're also a little brash."

Brash? Andie wasn't sure what that meant, but it didn't sound so good.

"You get along well with bold horses like Ranger," Mrs. Caufield continued. "Not flighty horses like Magic. As you ride him the next few weeks, you may decide that he's not the right horse for you."

"He *is* the right horse," Andie blurted.

Mrs. Caufield shrugged. "We'll see. Come on, let's try again." The riding director turned and walked back to the center of the ring.

Magic shifted his weight and shook his head, eager to get moving. Andie leaned over and stroked his neck.

"I'll do better, Mr. Magic," she promised him, "because I *know* you're the right horse for me."

Now all she had to do was prove it to everyone else.

"*That* disgusting thing is the project you're showing your parents this weekend?" Andie asked Mary Beth the next morning. She held up a jar filled with yellowish liquid. Something slimy with bulgy eyes was bobbing around in it.

The two girls were in Mary Beth's science classroom. Andie had stopped by so they could walk to lunch together.

"That disgusting thing is a dead frog," Mary Beth said shortly. Taking the jar from Andie, she set it back on the shelf with a dozen others. "Its name is Walter. I'm dissecting him this week."

Andie wrinkled her nose. "You're showing a cut-up frog to your parents? That's gross."

"It may be gross to you," Mary Beth said huffily as she walked back to her desk, "but our Parents' Project is supposed to be something neat we've been doing in one of our classes. And science is my favorite class."

"It would be," Andie muttered. She hated science and math and English and—well, just about every subject. But science was definitely the worst.

"So what are you showing your dad?" Mary Beth asked as she tucked her books into her backpack.

Andie shrugged. "I'm riding Magic. "

"Right, but you need something from one of your classes to show him, too," Mary Beth reminded her.

"I haven't thought of anything yet," Andie said. "I don't really have a favorite class."

"Well you have to do *something*," Mary Beth insisted. She slung her backpack over her shoulder, then followed Andie out the classroom door. "At Morning Meeting, Headmaster Frawley said—"

"Forget Frawley," Andie told her, pushing open the building door. Sunshine blasted in her face, making her squint. "I'll do something stupid, like read an essay I wrote in English."

Mary Beth started giggling. "Boy, I'd like to hear that one. 'Why I Hate School,' by Andie Break-All-the-Rules Perez."

Andie couldn't help but grin. "Pretty funny, Finney. So what are you doing for your riding project? Falling off Dan?"

Mary Beth ignored her. "Hey, here come Lauren and Jina. Lauren!" Mary Beth waved wildly.

Their roommates were walking across the courtyard, heading to the cafeteria in Eaton Hall. When Lauren saw Mary Beth and Andie, she waved back.

"So what are you doing, Finney?" Andie repeated. She jogged ahead of Mary Beth, then turned abruptly and started walking backward in front of her. She loved to bug Mary Beth about her lousy riding. "Lauren's doing some musical thing on Whisper and Jina's jumping that new pony."

Mary Beth flushed. "It's none of your business what I'm doing."

"Oh, come on," Andie persisted. "Tell me. I won't laugh."

"All right." Mary Beth stopped and eyed Andie warily. "You promise you won't laugh?"

Andie nodded eagerly. "Sure."

"I'm going to show my parents how I groom Dan and pick out his hooves."

"Pick out hooves!" Andie threw back her head and burst out laughing. "How stupid!"

Mary Beth scowled. "It is *not* stupid."

"Hey, what's so funny?" Lauren asked as she and Jina came up to them.

Lauren was wearing a heavy sweater over corduroy jeans. Jina wore a blue turtleneck under her navy wool Foxhall blazer. Her black hair was smoothed back in a hair band.

"Finney is," Andie gasped.

"Shut up, Andie," Mary Beth muttered. She

turned to Lauren. "So what's for lunch?"

"Tacos." Lauren smacked her lips. "My favorite."

"It's nice to see you're not still trying to starve yourself like Ashley," Andie said. "Speaking of which—"

She nudged Lauren with her elbow and pointed to the steps of Eaton Hall. Lauren, Jina, and Mary Beth all turned to follow her gaze.

A pretty, petite blond girl was standing in the middle of a group of older students. She was talking loudly and gesturing with one hand.

"Don't look now, but there's your friend," Andie whispered. "Who let her out of the nuthouse?"

"*Andie!*" Lauren hissed. "That's mean. And she wasn't in a nuthouse. She was in a hospital," she added, glaring at Andie.

Ashley Stewart had been Lauren's math tutor before midterm exams. When Lauren had realized that her new friend was losing too much weight, she'd finally had to tell someone, even though she'd promised Ashley she wouldn't. Now Ashley had returned from two weeks at a hospital where she'd been treated for an eating disorder called anorexia nervosa.

"Is this the first time you've seen Ashley since she came back to school?" Mary Beth asked Lauren.

Lauren nodded. "Yeah. The last time I talked with her on the phone, she didn't sound very friendly. She hated being in the hospital, and she was still saying it was all my fault she had to go there."

"I guess she thinks she has to blame someone," Jina said.

Andie had to agree. She wondered what the older girl would do when she saw Lauren.

Maybe there will be a fight, she thought hopefully. She couldn't help it. She liked Lauren a lot, but it wouldn't hurt to have a little excitement on campus. Life at school was so boring.

When Andie and her roommates reached the door to Eaton Hall, Ashley turned and looked over her shoulder at Lauren. Lauren stared dumbly back.

Andie gave her a little push. "Go say hi to Ashley. Tell her how *fat* she looks."

"Shut up, Andie." Lauren jerked away. "I like Ashley."

"Well, you're the only one who does," Jina

said under her breath. She still hadn't forgotten how mean Ashley had been to her when they'd competed in the same horse shows.

But Ashley just frowned and followed her friends into the cafeteria. "Well, Ashley doesn't seem to like *you* much," Mary Beth said to Lauren.

"So who cares who Ashley likes?" Andie said, "Let's go eat. If Ms. Skinnybones says anything nasty to you, Lauren, I'll dump taco sauce down her back."

Lauren swung around and glared at Andie. "Stay out of it, Andie. And quit saying such awful things about Ashley."

"Lauren's right," Jina said. "I'm not a big Ashley fan either, but she is sick with that eating disorder thing. You should lighten up, Andie."

"Really." Mary Beth frowned at Andie, too. "You've been cutting down just about everybody these last couple of days, Perez."

Andie threw up her hands. "Well, excu-u-u-se me. I can tell when I'm not wanted. I'll just go eat with somebody else." Spinning on her heels, she stomped up the steps.

Who do they think they are? Andie fumed as she jerked open the cafeteria door. Chin high,

28

she marched into the crowded lunchroom. Obviously, they weren't her friends.

She dropped her backpack on an empty table, trying not to notice as Lauren, Mary Beth, and Jina walked in a few minutes later. Their heads were bowed close together, as if they were talking about somebody.

Talking about *her.*

Which means they're definitely not my friends, Andie decided as she stomped over to the salad bar. Because there was no way friends would act so mean.

And that's fine with me, Andie thought darkly. *Let them be that way—I don't care.*

But deep inside, she did care. A lot.

"You are so-o-o beautiful," Andie crooned as she finished brushing Magic. She stepped back to admire her work. She'd spent a whole hour grooming the Thoroughbred. His mane was combed to one side, his hooves were polished, and his tail was brushed thick and full.

This is how he'll look on Saturday, Andie thought. *So my dad can see how perfect he is.*

Today was Tuesday. Only four more days until he came. Andie could hardly wait.

"Looking good," someone said. Dorothy Germaine, the stable manager, leaned over the Dutch door. Magic turned his head and eyed her calmly.

Andie smiled. Three weeks ago, someone coming up to the door would have startled him. "Thanks," she said to Dorothy. "Are you going to watch me today when I ride him?"

Dorothy nodded. She was a stocky woman in her forties who had worked with horses all her life. Her mud-stained sweatshirt pictured a horse leaping over a stone wall. The sweatshirt read GET A JUMP ON IT. "Mrs. Caufield is working with some riders who are doing a pairs routine for Saturday," Dorothy said. "She filled me in on what happened with you and Magic yesterday." She arched one brow. "Think you can handle His Highness today?"

"Yeah," Andie said sheepishly. "I've replayed the whole disaster in my mind about a hundred times so I know what *not* to do."

"Good," Dorothy said. "Longe him first for about fifteen minutes, then I'll be down."

When Dorothy left, Andie turned back to Magic. The handsome Thoroughbred rubbed his forehead against her arm. He wanted her to scratch him.

Andie stroked his star, then rubbed the inside of his ears. Magic wiggled his lips with pleasure.

Laughing, Andie buried her head in his sleek neck. "Today, I'm really ready to ride you," she told him. "I won't mess up this time and scare you, I promise."

Leaning back, she stared into Magic's dark, deep eyes. She really, really loved this horse. And soon he would be *her* horse.

That night, Andie hung around the dorm hall, watching the fourth floor's lone phone.

Ring! she muttered under her breath. *Ring!*

Study hour was over and her dad was supposed to call. In her bare feet, she paced to the end of the hall, spun around, then paced back to the open door of the suite.

When she glanced in the room, she could see Mary Beth, Lauren, and Jina stretched out on the floor. Her roommates were sorting through photographs that Mary Beth had taken over the last few weeks. They were putting them in an album to show their parents when they came this weekend.

Or something dumb like that. Andie couldn't remember exactly what her roommates were doing and she didn't care.

They weren't her friends anymore. Not that it mattered. When she'd ridden Magic today, he'd done pretty well, even though she'd still been a little nervous. And tonight her dad was going to call and tell her what time he was coming for Parents' Weekend.

That was what mattered.

Bri-i-ing. The sudden jangling of the phone made Andie jump. Twirling around, she raced to answer it. Two other girls dashed from their rooms, but Andie beat them to it.

"Hello?" she gasped into the receiver.

"Uh, hi," a male voice said.

A wimpy male voice. Andie bet it was Tommy, that dorky sixth-grader from the Manchester School. For some strange reason he liked Mary Beth, and she'd said he was supposed to call her tonight.

"Is this Captain Tommy?" Andie asked, her tone sarcastic.

"Uh, yeah. Is Mary Beth there?"

Andie let out a disgusted snort. No! she was about to shout and hang up. But Mary Beth had run out into the hall and was looking at her expectantly.

Andie rolled her eyes. "Yes, she's here," she said sweetly, "only she's on the toilet. I'll have to call her."

Mary Beth's face grew bright red. "Andie!" she screeched as she darted to the phone and jerked the receiver from Andie's hand.

Andie burst out laughing. Jina and Lauren were standing in the doorway now, looking accusingly at her. But Andie couldn't help it. Andie laughed so hard, tears filled her eyes.

Mary Beth turned her back on her, trying to hear what Tommy was saying.

"Just hurry up, Finney," Andie said loudly. "I'm waiting for an *important* call."

Mary Beth glared at Andie over her shoulder. Andie glared right back, then stomped to the end of the hall.

She crossed her arms in front of her chest and leaned against the wall. Lauren was still standing in the doorway, looking dopey. She wore fuzzy slippers that had ears like puppies, and a flannel nightgown. She was staring at Andie.

"What are you looking at?" Andie snapped.

Lauren just shook her head and went back into the suite. Mary Beth was giggling away on the phone.

Andie rolled her eyes. What could wimpy Tommy possibly be saying that was funny?

Five minutes went by. Andie shifted nervously from foot to foot. If Mary Beth didn't get off that phone soon, it would be lights-out. Her father knew she couldn't come to the phone after ten. And tomorrow he was going out of town on a business trip.

She had to talk to him tonight!

Angrily, Andie marched toward Mary Beth. "Hang up!" she mouthed.

Mary Beth nodded, then turned away. Andie couldn't stand it any longer. Reaching over Mary Beth's shoulder, she pushed down the switchhook, cutting off the call.

Mary Beth's mouth fell open. She spun around, looking furious. "What did you do *that* for?"

"You talked long enough," Andie said. "I've got to call my father."

"Well, you could have asked *nicely*," Mary Beth sputtered. "I would have said good-bye."

"Sure you would have." Andie took the receiver from Mary Beth and started to dial.

Her father's home phone rang. *Be there*, Andie whispered to herself.

"Hello—"

"Dad? It's me, Andie," she blurted into the phone.

"This is Ramon Perez. I'm sorry I can't speak with you—"

Andie inhaled sharply. It was her father's answering machine! He wasn't home. Or, she corrected herself, he wasn't answering.

Quickly, she pushed the switchhook down

and dialed her father's office, only to reach another answering machine.

She couldn't believe it. He'd definitely said he was going to call. Maybe she could reach him on his car phone.

It took Andie ten minutes to find her father's cellular phone number on her messy desk. Finally, she found it, stuck to the lollipop that had been sitting there since Sunday night. Mary Beth, Jina, and Lauren didn't even look up as she dashed back out the door.

She dialed the phone with trembling fingers. Her father's number rang once, twice, three times.

He wasn't in his car, either.

Slowly, Andie hung up the phone. It was almost ten o'clock. He hadn't called.

Even though he'd promised.

Tears of anger pricked Andie's eyes. She swiped at them with the palm of her hand, then raced down the hall to the stairs. Her bare feet pounding the polished wood, she leaped down the stairs until she reached the front door.

She yanked it open and ran outside, hardly noticing the cold night air. Wrapping her arms around her chest, she sat down on the stone steps.

Soon she began to shiver. Teeth chattering, she tucked her hands into the sleeves of her sweatshirt and huddled into a ball.

In five minutes, it would be lights-out. Andie knew she would have to be back in her room by then, in bed. Otherwise, she'd get in big trouble with Ms. Shiroo, the dorm mother.

But right now, Andie didn't care.

She didn't care about anything.

Andie heard the heavy door open behind her.

"Psst, *Andie*," someone said.

That someone sounded a lot like nosy Lauren.

Andie tucked her feet underneath her. They were freezing. "What do you want?" she said, without turning around.

"It's almost lights-out."

"So what." Andie looked up at the sky. Zillions of stars were twinkling, and through the canopy of leaves she could just make out the Big Dipper.

"You have to come in!" Lauren insisted.

"And *you* have to mind your own business," Andie shot back.

Lauren gave a little gasp, and Andie

hunched lower. She knew Lauren was just trying to be nice. Then why was she, Andie, being so mean?

The door shut. Lauren had gone away. For a moment, Andie sat shivering in the cold, feeling rotten.

Suddenly, someone sat down beside her. Andie drew away, startled.

Lauren smiled apologetically. "Sorry if I scared you." She'd thrown a bathrobe over her nightgown.

Andie set her chin down on her knees and wrapped her arms around her legs. "You didn't scare me."

"So what are you doing out here?" Lauren asked, clutching her robe tighter around her.

"Nothing."

"It's got to be something," Lauren pressed. "You've been really crabby the last couple of days."

I have not, Andie was about to say. But she knew Lauren was right.

"Is Magic doing okay?" Lauren asked.

Andie nodded. "Pretty good." She stared at her roommate's fuzzy slippers. They had soulful puppy eyes, floppy ears, and button noses.

She almost wanted to pat them.

"Was your dad supposed to call tonight?" Lauren persisted.

Andie's fingers tightened around her ankles. "No," she said quickly. There was no way she wanted anyone to know that her father didn't care about her.

"That's what you told Mary Beth."

"Well, I forgot. He's on a business trip," she fibbed.

Lauren sighed. "You know, Andie, you don't always have to act so tough." She stood up and the puppies' ears flopped.

Yes I do. Andie answered silently, burying her head between her knees. *That way things don't hurt as much.*

"I mean, Jina and Mary Beth and I would like to be your friends, only—" Lauren hesitated, "—only sometimes you make it real hard."

A tear rolled down Andie's cheek and splashed on the cold stone. Quickly, she covered the wet spot with her foot. Lauren waited for a moment, then turned to go back into the dorm.

Andie knew she had to say something

before Lauren left. Something to show that her roommates *were* important to her.

She twisted around on the step. "I know!" she blurted out.

Lauren paused in the lighted doorway, looking confused.

Andie took a deep breath. "I know I'm not always a great friend," she said, slower this time. "And—and I'm sorry."

A smile spread slowly over Lauren's face. She was about to say something when Mary Beth flung the door open with a bang. "Andie!" Mary Beth gasped, out of breath from running down four flights of stairs. "There's a phone call for you. I think it's your dad!"

Andie jumped up. Her dad!

She grinned broadly at Lauren and Mary Beth, then dashed into the dorm, taking the stairs two at a time.

"How about trotting from corner to corner when the song gets to that faster part?" Andie suggested to Lauren. It was Thursday afternoon, and the two of them were standing by the entrance to the outdoor dressage ring.

Lauren wore her riding clothes, down vest, and helmet. She held her horse, Whisper, who was tacked up.

Andie rewound the tape and played the part of the song that she was talking about. It was by their favorite group, the Renegades. Lauren and Whisper were going to "dance" to the music.

Lauren nodded. "Yeah. That might work." Then she sighed. "It's not like I know how to do all those fancy pirouettes and flying changes that they do at the Grand Prix musical freestyle level. I guess a trot will have to do."

"You can still make it interesting." Andie pointed to the M marker at the opposite end of the ring. "Trot to there, then canter to F when the beat gets faster—"

"Then I can make circles in each corner!" Lauren cut in, getting more excited. "And when the beat slows down, I can slow to a collected trot."

"Right." Andie turned off the player and rewound the tape again.

Whisper pricked her ears at the whirring noise. Lauren patted her soothingly.

"Don't worry, your parents will love anything you do," Andie told her roommate. "But remember, you only have today and tomorrow left to practice. Ready to try it?"

Lauren nodded. "At least it won't be as hard as a dressage test. If I forget something, I can just make it up as I go along."

"Right." Andie set the tape player down, then gave her friend a leg up.

When Lauren was settled in the saddle, she grinned down at Andie. "Thanks for all the help."

Andie shrugged. "It's no big deal."

"It is to me." Lauren squeezed her legs against Whisper's sides, and the two moved into the dressage ring.

Andie turned on the tape and watched as Whisper broke into a smooth, flowing trot. Her thoughts began to stray back to her dad's phone call Tuesday night. He had called just in time, all apologies. He was coming to Foxhall for tomorrow night's hello dinner. Then he was staying at a nearby motel until Sunday.

Andie was excited. But she was also a little nervous.

Ever since she could remember, she and her

dad had had trouble getting along. This would be their first chance to really spend some time together.

She hoped the visit would work out.

"How am I doing?" Lauren called over the music.

Andie snapped back to attention. "Maybe begin cantering at M and cross diagonally to V or something," she called back.

Lauren nodded, and Andie watched her and Whisper break into a canter. She knew that Lauren and Mary Beth were really excited about their parents coming for the weekend, too. Even Jina was looking forward to it, now that she knew for sure her mom was coming without her usual secretaries and assistants.

"Hi, Andie." Mary Beth came up to the dressage ring leading Dangerous Dan, the huge horse she rode for lessons. "So what do you think?"

Proudly, Mary Beth showed off Dan. The part-draft horse was too clunky to look beautiful, but Mary Beth had really polished him up. Except for his mane.

Andie frowned as she eyed it. The part near his withers had been shortened to about four inches long, so it lay flat and even on his neck.

But the other half was still long and shaggy.

"What did you do to his mane?" Andie asked.

Mary Beth grimaced. "Well, I started to pull it. Jina showed me how. I did a little every day, but…" Her voice trailed away as she held out her index finger of her right hand. It was covered with Band-Aids. "I wore all the skin off my finger, and now it hurts too much to finish. Besides, Dan doesn't like it when I pull his hair. He keeps shaking his head—" she took a deep breath "—and Jina's at Middlefield Stables so she can't help, but grooming Dan is my special project and now he looks so silly and I don't want my family seeing him like *this* and—"

As Mary Beth took another breath, her eyes darted to Andie, as if she were waiting for a snide comment.

"Why don't you use a pulling comb?" Andie suggested.

Mary Beth gave her a blank look. "A what?"

"A pulling comb," Andie repeated. "Ask Dorothy. She probably has a thinning knife, too. I'll show you how to use them."

"You will?" Mary Beth sounded totally shocked.

Andie nodded. "Sure. We'll get his mane done in a jiffy. Jina probably didn't think about using them because Superstar's mane is so wispy, she doesn't need them."

"Gee, that'd be great," Mary Beth said eagerly. "Are you *sure* you want to help?"

Andie nodded again. "Yep. After Lauren finishes, I'll meet you at Dan's stall."

"Thanks," Mary Beth said, staring at Andie in disbelief.

Andie turned her attention back to Lauren. Whisper had halted. Now Lauren was backing the mare up as the song came to an end. When the tape clicked off, Lauren bowed low in the saddle.

Andie and Mary Beth clapped and whistled.

"That was nice of you to help Lauren," Mary Beth said to Andie as she started to leave with Dan.

Andie just grinned.

She *was* being nice. For a change.

And it actually felt kind of good.

6

"So how do I look?" Andie asked Jina on Friday afternoon. The two girls were dressing for the hello dinner that night. For once they didn't have to wear their stupid Foxhall blazers. They could wear anything they wanted.

"Wow." Jina's eyes widened. "You look, um—" She hesitated.

Andie touched her hair nervously. She'd pulled the long, wild strands back with a gold barrette. Turning, she checked her image in the mirror.

"I look what—?" Andie prompted. Jina was always honest. "Too much makeup? Is my skirt too short?"

Jina hesitated. "Well—I guess I'm just not used to seeing you all dressed up. You look so much older."

"Older's okay," Andie replied, anxiously tugging on her skirt. "But maybe this is too short. You know fathers—"

Oops. Andie glanced over at Jina. *What a stupid thing to say.* Jina had never mentioned a father. Andie didn't even know if she had one.

Jina ignored the comment. "Yeah, it is pretty short."

"I'll change it then." Andie began to yank off the skirt. "Where's Lauren and Mary Beth?"

"Meeting their parents in the Common Room," Jina said, sounding a little sad. Her mom wasn't arriving until Saturday. "You'd better hurry and get dressed," she added. "They're all coming up here to see the suite."

"Terrific," Andie muttered as she pulled another skirt off a hanger. She could already hear Mary Beth's voice coming down the hall. "All we need is Finney's whole family stuffed in here."

Quickly, Andie stepped into the skirt. She was just pulling up the zipper when three kids burst through the door and raced into the room.

"Is this it, Mary Beth? Is this it?" one of the kids cried as he whirled around and dashed back out into the hall.

The other two stopped and stared at Andie and Jina. One was a little girl around three who suddenly leaped toward Andie and grabbed her around the legs.

"You must be Lauwen," she squealed. Andie grimaced as the little girl smiled up at her. Her red hair was pulled into a ponytail that stuck off the top of her head. A faint spray of freckles covered her nose.

Oh, no, Andie thought, *a miniature Mary Beth.*

"No, I'm—"

"You're Jina then, right?" the older boy asked. Frowning, he stepped right up to Andie and eyed her seriously. He was around nine and had such short hair, Andie couldn't tell what color it was. But his cheeks and arms were covered with so many freckles they looked like splashes of paint.

Andie gave Jina a desperate look, but her roommate just giggled.

"No, I'm not Jina, I'm—"

"Mom, Dad, here it is!" Mary Beth called, bursting into the room. Waving her arm grandly, she ushered her parents into the suite. Mary Beth's mother was plump with red hair permed into short curls. She was smiling, and

49

her entire face was covered with freckles. Mr. Finney came in right behind her. He was tall and skinny and had to duck his balding head to get in the door.

"Woof!"

"Dogums!" the little girl cried in delight.

A hairy beast bounded past the Finneys and into the room, a leash attached to his neck. A boy about seven years old was attached to the other end of the leash. Mary Beth's little sister loosened her hold on Andie's legs and lunged for the dog as he leaped toward them.

Andie jumped out of the way, but she wasn't fast enough. The hairy thing reared up. Tongue lolling, it greeted her with a slobbery kiss, then jumped down and dashed for Jina's bed.

"Dogums, no!" Mary Beth hollered, diving for the leash. She tumbled over her brother and sister and the three of them fell on the floor.

Dogums jumped onto Jina's bed, circled twice, and flopped down. Then, panting, he stared up at everyone. At least Andie thought he was staring. He had so much hair, she couldn't see his eyes.

"Dogums, get down," Mary Beth commanded as she struggled to her feet. She tugged hard on the leash, but Dogums didn't budge.

Jina had a funny look on her face. The dog had gotten mud and dog hair all over her bed. Still, she sat down next to the furry beast and began to pat him hesitantly.

"Oh, Bethie," Mrs. Finney exclaimed, clasping her hands. She was circling the room, touching all the furniture as if nothing had even happened. "Your suite is so-o-o-o-o cute. Just how I imagined it. It was hard to tell on the first day—"

"Mom, Dad, meet Jina and Andie," Mary Beth interrupted. Grinning from ear to ear, Mary Beth introduced her roommates. "And this is Benji." She pointed to the older boy. "And Reed." That was the one still clutching the dog's leash. "And Tammy." Obviously, the little sister.

Andie smiled numbly at Mary Beth's family. She couldn't believe it—every single Finney had freckles.

"Oh, I am so *delighted* to meet you both!" Mrs. Finney reached out and pulled Andie close in a big hug.

Andie's mouth fell open in surprise. Mrs. Finney was squeezing her to death.

"Mary Beth has told us so much about you girls," Mrs. Finney cooed. She held Andie at arm's length, inspecting her. Then she turned and, bending over the bed, hugged Jina, who blushed with embarrassment.

"Yup, nice place, Mary Beth," Mr. Finney said, nodding. Hands shoved in his pants pockets, he surveyed the room. "A little crowded, though."

Especially with all of you in here, Andie wanted to say. There were Finneys everywhere. "Psst, hey, I gotta go to the bathroom!" Someone tugged on Andie's skirt.

Andie looked down. Tammy was hopping from foot to foot, an anxious expression on her face. "It's right in there." Andie pointed to the bathroom door.

"You come with me," Tammy insisted.

"Me? No way. Your mom or dad can take you." Andie glanced over at the Finneys. Mary Beth was chattering away as she showed her mom and dad her textbooks. Jina, Reed, and Benji were all patting Dogums.

"*Please*," Tammy insisted.

"Oh, all right." She led Tammy into the bathroom and helped her unsnap her pants. Reed popped his head inside the doorway.

"Whatcha doing?" he asked.

"What does it look like?" Andie asked.

"Hey, is that the shower?"

He ran over to the shower stall and began fiddling with the knobs. All of a sudden, water began to spray everywhere.

"Would you turn that off!" Andie hollered. "Then *leave*."

"Sure." Reed cranked off the water and gave Andie a knowing look. "Now I know which one you are. You're the bossy one."

"And you're the bratty one," Andie shot back.

"Ha." Reed stuck out his tongue at her before disappearing out the door.

"He is a bwat," Tammy said solemnly.

Oh great. Andie groaned as she leaned back against the wall. Thank goodness her father was going to be here before dinner. Then she could escape. She didn't think she could stand the Finney tribe one more minute.

"Andie?" a soft voice came from the doorway.

"What?" Andie whirled around.

Jina was looking in, an apologetic smile on her face. "Uh, Dean Wilkes wants to see you."

Andie's brows shot up. "Dean Wilkes? What does she want?"

"She has a message from your dad," Jina explained. "He called the dean. Something about having to work late. You're supposed to go to her office."

Andie froze against the wall.

"Okay?" Jina asked anxiously.

Andie nodded slowly. "Sure."

"What's wrong?" Tammy asked when Jina had left.

Andie swallowed hard. "Nothing." She bent down to help Tammy pull up her pants. "Can you keep a secret?"

Tammy's eyes widened. "I love secwets."

"I'm not going to see Dean Wilkes," Andie said, "because I already know what she wants to tell me."

"What?"

"My dad's not coming tonight for the hello dinner."

"Weally? That's too bad." Tammy's mouth drooped. Then she held up both arms. "Would a hug make you feel better?"

Andie shrugged, then smiled sadly. "Nah. Thanks anyway, but I feel fine. After all, I'm used to it."

She was used to her dad breaking his promises.

But it still hurt.

7

"Andie!" Lauren called from the Common Room as Andie came down the dorm stairs. "I want you to meet my mom and dad."

Andie gritted her teeth. *Great.* She didn't think she could stand another disgustingly happy family.

Plastering a fake smile on her face, Andie turned into the large room. It was filled with students and parents eating cheese and crackers and chattering away as they waited for dinner.

Lauren grabbed Andie's hand and pulled her across the room. Her petite roommate had brushed out her long, blond hair so it hung down her back. She wore stockings, flats, and a flower-print dress.

Andie had never seen Lauren so dressed

up. She looked sickeningly girly and cute.

"Why do you have on your coat already?" Lauren asked as she led Andie through the crowded room. "Dinner won't be for fifteen minutes."

"I'm cold," Andie fibbed. There was no way she was going to tell Lauren the real reason.

"And why are you wearing your barn boots?" Lauren added, frowning as she looked down at Andie's feet.

"Would you quit being so nosy?" Andie snapped. "Just hurry up and introduce me to your parents."

Lauren's cheeks reddened. "You don't have to get so mad."

Lauren stopped in front of a sofa where her sister, Stephanie, was sitting on the arm, talking to two grown-ups. Immediately, the man stood and extended his hand.

"Hi, I'm Dale Remick, Lauren and Stephanie's dad," he said, shaking Andie's hand heartily.

As if I couldn't tell, Andie thought. He looked just like Stephanie—tall, tan, and blond.

"And I'm Lauren's mother," said a pretty woman with dark blond hair turned under in a sleek pageboy. She was dressed in a stylish navy suit and matching heels. "We're so glad to meet one of Lauren's roommates," she added, giving her daughter an affectionate squeeze.

"It's nice to meet you, too." Andie smiled politely.

Stephanie suddenly jumped off the arm of the chair, waving to someone on the other side of the room. "Oh, look, there's *my* roommate, Christina," she said.

Andie figured this was her chance to disappear. The sooner she got away, the better. She didn't want anyone asking about her father.

"See you at dinner," Andie whispered to Lauren and slipped into the crowd.

But she knew it was a lie. There was no way she was going to sit through a whole dinner listening to someone else's father gush over his daughter.

Quickly, Andie ran outside. A cold rain was falling.

Now what? she asked herself impatiently. It was miserable outside. Should she go see Dean Wilkes?

No. She didn't need to hear again that her father wasn't coming tonight.

And she couldn't go back into the dorm

and face the Finneys and the Remicks. She'd just have to find someplace to hang out until everybody left for dinner. Then she could sneak back into the suite. No one would even miss her.

Flipping the hood of her coat over her head, Andie ran across the courtyard. It was last year's coat and the sleeves were too short.

If my mom were here, we could go shopping, Andie thought as raindrops pelted her cheeks. *But Mom isn't here either,* she reminded herself. *Just like Dad.* But at least her mother had a lame excuse. She was out of the country.

Andie reached the stone archway that connected the administration building to the library and dropped down on a nearby bench. Cold water soaked through her skirt.

Jumping up quickly, she gave the wet bench a disgusted kick. In the distance, she could see people with umbrellas hurrying across the courtyard toward Eaton Hall. It wouldn't be long before she could sneak back into the suite.

She shivered as a damp wind whistled down the hill and rain whipped through the arch. Her wet bottom and stockinged legs were freezing. All she could do was watch impatiently as several more groups of students and parents straggled across the courtyard.

Andie stamped her feet, trying to warm them. Water splashed up her legs.

This isn't working, she decided suddenly. By the time all the families left Bracken Hall, she'd be frozen solid.

She turned and peered up the hill. She could just make out the outline of the main barn silhouetted in the mercury-vapor light that shone from the lone pole. The barn wasn't very far. She could hide in Magic's stall, where it would be warm and dry.

Only you'd be breaking another stupid Foxhall rule, Andie told herself, *big time.* Students were allowed at the stables only at certain hours.

But who would know?

Who would care?

Clutching the hood tightly around her neck, Andie raced up the hill into the dark, rainy night.

Halfway up, she slipped in the mud, nearly falling, but she caught herself just in time. When she finally reached the barn, she flattened herself against a shadowy wall. Cautiously, she peered down the outside aisle toward the office door. It was closed and no light shone underneath it. No one was around.

Andie breathed a sigh of relief as she made her way under the overhang to Magic's stall. The top door was shut tight against the nasty weather.

"Magic?" Andie called softly as she slowly unlatched both doors. She swung open the top.

The Thoroughbred snorted. Straw rustled as he came over to Andie. When the light hit his eyes, he blinked sleepily.

Andie stroked his soft nose. "Did I wake you up?"

Opening the bottom door, she slipped inside. The stall was dry and smelled like fresh hay. Magic looked at her curiously, then ducked his head into his feed bucket and licked the bottom.

"No, it's not time for breakfast yet," Andie told him as she latched the bottom door behind her. Then she swung the top door toward her so it was almost closed.

The stall was dark. No one would even know she was there.

Andie's heart thumped as she thought about the trouble she'd be in if someone *did* find her here. The barn was off limits after six o'clock unless a student had special permission. Andie tried to remember what would happen if she was caught. Would she get kicked out of Foxhall? She was already on probation.

Her stomach lurched. A month ago, she'd wanted to get kicked out of school. But now that she had Magic, she wanted to stay at Foxhall.

So why was she hiding out at the stables? Why take the chance of getting expelled?

There was only one answer: There was nowhere else to go.

Andie rested her forehead against Magic's neck and laced her fingers in his mane. He'd grabbed a bite of hay and was chewing slowly. Andie's stomach growled hungrily.

But there was no way she was going to dinner. She didn't care if she starved to death. She couldn't stand making polite conversation with Mary Beth's or Lauren's family. She couldn't stand telling everyone that her father wasn't coming. Everyone would feel sorry for her, like they did for Jina. But Jina's mom was arriving tomorrow. Myra Golden hadn't broken any promise to *her* daughter.

A sudden noise outside made Andie freeze.

Magic stopped chewing and pricked his ears toward the sound.

Someone was walking slowly down the aisle, shoes shuffling against the concrete. Andie held her breath and clutched Magic's mane tightly.

Whoever it was would see Magic's open top door. They'd know someone was inside.

The footsteps drew closer.

Andie's stomach tightened into a hard knot.

She was going to get caught!

8

I have to hide! Andie thought wildly. Her gaze darted around the stall. The corner to her left was the darkest. Even if the person swung open the top door, it would still be bathed in shadows.

It was her only chance.

Andie patted Magic's neck, then tiptoed to the corner. Straw crinkled with her every step. When she reached the corner, she crouched down against the wall. A cobweb grabbed her ear.

She swatted at the sticky strands. Then the squeak of a hinge made her catch her breath.

Someone was opening the stall door!

Andie buried her head in her arms, trying to make herself as small as possible. Maybe, by some miracle, the person wouldn't see her.

Then Magic began to move toward her. Stretching out his neck, he lowered his head and sniffed her hood. *Go away!* Andie wanted to shout.

The top door creaked open. Light washed across the straw.

Don't look over here, Andie pleaded silently. She held her breath. Someone was definitely looking in. She could hear the person breathing.

Just then, Magic pawed the ground inches from Andie's foot.

Andie squinched her eyes tight and clasped her hands hard around her legs. This was it. Any second now, the person would see her.

"Andie?" a voice called softly.

Was that Jina?

Andie poked her head up. Jina's golden eyes peered anxiously into the corner. Then she spotted Andie.

"It *is* you!" she gasped, sounding relieved. Unlatching the bottom door, she stepped into the stall. She wore a long raincoat over her slacks, and her dressy shoes were muddy.

"Whoa, Magic." Jina shut the door behind

her, then patted his neck. He moved over toward his hay net. "Are you all right?" she asked Andie, crouching next to her.

Andie let out her breath. "Yes, now that I know it was you sneaking around out there. You scared me to death!"

"Well, *you* scared *me* when you didn't show up for dinner!" Jina said, anger creeping into her voice. "I thought you went to see Dean Wilkes, but when she came into the cafeteria without you, I got worried."

"Why?" Andie asked.

"Because I didn't know where you were!" Jina exclaimed. Then she glanced nervously over her shoulder. "Do you know how much trouble we're going to get in if we're caught up here?" she said.

Andie sighed. "Yeah. Only I just didn't know what else to do." She frowned at Jina. "You should go back to dinner. I don't need you getting in trouble, too."

Jina pressed her lips together and frowned. "It's a little late to think about that now." She stood up quickly. "Sometimes you are so selfish, Andie."

Andie's mouth dropped open. "Me?"

"Yes, *you*. Do you think you're the only girl in Foxhall who doesn't have a parent with her tonight? Do you think you're the only one whose mother or father couldn't make it?"

"Well, I—I—" Andie stuttered. Why was Jina yelling at her?

"Well, you're not," Jina said. Hands on hips, she glared down at Andie. "But you *are* the only one who's acting like a total baby about it."

Andie bristled. "A *baby!*"

"That's right. My mother isn't here and you don't see *me* hiding in a stall."

Andie jumped up, too. "That's because *your* mother wasn't supposed to come tonight. She didn't break *her* promise."

"How do you know?" Jina snapped, her nose inches from Andie's. "You were too busy worrying about your own selfish self!"

"I was not!" Andie hollered, but she knew Jina was right. Jina was alone tonight, too, and Andie hadn't even cared.

Suddenly Jina's shoulders drooped like a deflating balloon. "I'm sorry," she said. "I know how you feel. I shouldn't have yelled at you."

"No, you shouldn't have," Andie said. Then

she grinned. "But I deserved it."

Jina bit her lip. "Well, if we do get in trouble, I really will get mad."

"Come on, then. Let's get back to Eaton Hall before someone finds us." Andie pushed Jina toward the door. Magic thrust his nose into Andie's shoulder.

"Good night, Magic." She kissed the Thoroughbred on the nose. "We have to go."

Jina unlatched the door. She checked to the right, then the left. "All clear," she whispered, slipping into the aisle.

Andie started to giggle. In her long raincoat, Jina looked like a spy in a movie.

"Shhh." Jina frowned and pressed a finger to her lips.

Andie latched both doors behind her, then tiptoed after Jina, exaggerating her steps like a cartoon character.

"Maybe we should say good-bye to Superstar, too," Andie whispered, "in case Headmonster Frawley catches us and throws us in jail—forever."

Jina shot her an annoyed look. She obviously didn't think this sneaking around stuff was very funny.

When they reached Eaton Hall, both girls

were soaked and muddy. Behind them, a few latecomers were still making their way across the misty courtyard.

Jina let out a huge sigh of relief. "We made it. Let's just hope no one asks why we're so late and smell like horses." She started up the steps.

Andie shoved her hands in her coat pockets and watched as her roommate opened the door to the cafeteria. Sounds of laughter and clinking silverware floated down the steps.

"Aren't you coming?" Jina asked.

Andie shook her head. "No. You go on. I'm not hungry."

Jina frowned. For a moment, she studied Andie, then nodded her head as if she understood. "Okay. I'll bring you a roll."

Andie smiled. "Thanks. And Jina—I'm sorry about your mom. You know, about her not being here for the hello dinner."

Jina shrugged. "I'm used to it."

Andie knew her roommate was lying. Nobody got used to it.

As soon as Jina disappeared into the cafeteria, Andie turned and headed quickly toward Bracken Hall. She felt better about her father not coming for the dinner. Now all she wanted to do was change into her warm nightie and snuggle under the covers with the latest teen magazine.

But when she opened the door to suite 4B, her nose wrinkled. It smelled like a stinky dog. She was glad Dogums had chosen Jina's bed and not hers. Then she noticed all the pillows scattered on the floor. The Finney brats must have had a pillow fight.

Disgusted, Andie picked her own pillow up and tossed it on her bed. She was just unbuttoning her wet coat when someone knocked on the door.

Startled, she turned around. Dean Wilkes was standing in the doorway.

"May I come in, Ms. Perez?"

Andie gulped. For a second, she thought about saying no, but she quickly realized that would be a stupid mistake.

The stern expression on Dean Wilkes's face told her she was already in enough trouble.

9

"Wilkes gave you *trash* detail?" Lauren asked Andie the next morning. She was sitting on the edge of her bed, pulling on her high, black riding boots.

Andie nodded. "Yep. This morning I have to pick up every piece of wet garbage from the courtyard."

"Oo-ooh. That's nasty," Mary Beth said. She was already dressed. "I'd help except in five minutes I'm meeting my family for breakfast. They're really excited about seeing *Dangerous Dan*." She giggled.

Jina stood in the bathroom doorway, towel drying her hair. She wore breeches and a turtleneck. "I'd help, too, but my mom should be here any minute."

"Ditto." Lauren stomped her heel on the

floor, then reached for her navy wool hunt coat. "Stephanie and I are having breakfast with Mom and Dad, and then we're all going up to the stables."

Andie sighed. "That's all right, guys. I didn't expect any help. I mean, it's my own stupid fault I got caught skipping the dinner."

"Well, at least that's all you got caught doing." Jina gave Andie a knowing look, then went back into the bathroom.

"What did she mean by that?" Mary Beth asked.

"Nothing." Andie stood up and pulled on her jeans. Her father wasn't coming until after lunch, and there was no reason to put on something nice to pick up trash. "I just hope there aren't any smelly baby diapers out there."

Lauren giggled. "You think of the grossest things, Andie. Come on, Mary Beth, I'll walk downstairs with you."

"See you two guys later," Mary Beth called as they went out the door.

Andie pulled a sweatshirt over her head, then stared out the window. It was going to be a gorgeous morning. Too gorgeous to pick up trash. She should be at the stables, grooming Magic.

"Are you ready yet, Jinaki?" Andie hollered over her shoulder.

"Yeah." Jina came into the room, twisting a Scrunchie around her ponytail. "Do you see my mom's car, yet?"

Andie shook her head. "No limo. Just a bright red sports car. It's pulling up to the parking lot beside the dorm."

Jina broke into a big smile. "Great! That means my mom drove by herself. Jamison won't be around to bug her every minute about phone calls and work."

Andie leaned closer to the window. "That fancy car is your *mom's?*"

Jina joined her. "Yup."

A handsome black woman had opened the door and was climbing out of the driver's seat. She wore a black leather jacket, matching skirt, dark nylons, and ankle boots. Jina knocked on the glass and waved excitedly.

Grinning broadly, the woman waved back.

Jina grabbed her coat off her bed. "See you at breakfast," she called as she hurried into the hall.

"Yeah, right," Andie muttered. She slumped back onto her bed and idly picked at the fuzz on the blanket.

Now that her roommates were gone, it was horribly quiet in the suite. And lonely. She wouldn't even mind a visit from Tammy, Reed, or Dogums.

Bending down, Andie fished her sneakers out from under the bed. Dustballs clung to the laces. She put them on, then pulled a hooded sweatshirt over her other sweatshirt.

It was going to be a long morning.

Twenty minutes later, Andie munched on the last bite of a Danish as she halfheartedly speared wadded-up paper with a stick she'd found. Ugh. She wrinkled her nose as she dropped the paper into a plastic trash bag. The stuff she was finding in the courtyard was disgusting, especially after all that rain last night.

A group of students hurried past her on their way to the gym. An exhibition swim meet was being held for the parents. The girls glanced over their shoulders at Andie, then started giggling. One of the girls dropped a gum wrapper on purpose. Andie stuck out her tongue at their departing backs.

With another sigh she put her hands on her

hips, and surveyed the courtyard. Soggy white blobs dotted the grass everywhere. She'd never get finished.

I have to finish, Andie thought. *I've got to groom Magic before my father comes.*

With a sigh, she headed for a stray paper cup. Then something darting around the bushes in front of the library caught her eye. A big dog romped into view. Dogums!

Andie braced herself. Then she saw Tammy, Reed, and Benji duck in and out of the bushes. Mary Beth was with them.

"What are you guys doing?" Andie called.

"Woof!" Dogums leaped in the air, dragging Mary Beth from the bushes. His muddy paws missed Andie's leg by inches.

"We're picking up twash!" Tammy said excitedly. She held up a handful of gray notebook paper. "It's fun."

"Fun?" Andie wrinkled her nose.

Mary Beth smiled sheepishly. "I told my brothers and sister that we helped clean up the courtyard *every* morning."

"We do?" Andie asked, puzzled. Then it dawned on her what Mary Beth was doing. "Oh, *right*. We do." Andie nodded emphatically.

"How's this, guys?" someone said.

Lauren walked around the corner of the library carrying a plastic bag.

"Oops," she said when she saw Andie.

"It was supposed to be a surprise," Mary Beth explained. "We also didn't want Dean Wilkes to find out we were helping you."

Just then, Benji and Reed ran up and stuffed paper in Andie's bag.

"We got everything by the cafeteria," Benji said proudly.

Andie stared at her roommates and the younger kids. She didn't know what to say.

Tammy sidled closer to Andie and slipped her hand in hers. "Let's pick up some more," she said. "This is lots of fun."

Andie glanced down at Mary Beth's little sister, then over at Reed and Benji. Their freckly faces were crinkled in big grins. Maybe they weren't such brats after all.

"Thanks, guys," Andie said finally, giving everyone a big smile. "With all your help, I'll definitely have time to get Magic ready for my dad!"

He'll be here any second, Andie told herself nervously as she leaned on the rail around the outdoor ring that afternoon. Mary Beth's and Lauren's families were standing behind her. They were all watching Lauren and Whisper finish their musical freestyle performance.

Andie glanced anxiously toward the parking lot. She tensed as a dark blue car drove in. Was that her father's rental car?

A woman climbed out, and Andie groaned loudly.

"Shhh," Stephanie hushed. "I can't hear the music."

Andie turned back to watch Lauren. She was cantering Whisper in a small circle at the opposite end of the ring. Then Whisper changed leads in mid-stride and started in the other direction to form a figure eight.

Lauren's mom and dad clapped heartily. Andie knew Lauren had practiced that pattern a hundred times. She was glad it had worked out well.

As the music stopped, Lauren halted Whisper in the middle of the ring and bowed.

"Bravo! Bravo!" her dad called.

Mrs. Remick clapped loudly, but Stephanie seemed less enthusiastic. Andie figured the older girl was jealous of all the attention her sister was getting.

Another car drove into the parking lot. Andie held her breath. A tall, slender man wearing a bulky sweater stepped out. He had black hair laced with gray.

"My father's here!" Andie squealed as Lauren rode Whisper out the gate.

"Dad!" she hollered, waving frantically. He waved back, then started up the drive to the stables.

"I want you all to meet him," Andie gushed to everyone around her. "Mr. and Mrs. Remick and Mr. and Mrs. Finney, and Reed and Benji and Tammy and—"

Andie looked around for Mary Beth and Tammy, but she didn't see them. Benji was standing next to his dad holding Dogums. Reed was perched on the top rail of the fence. Mrs. Finney was with the Remicks congratulating Lauren. Mary Beth and Tammy were gone.

Andie grabbed Stephanie's hand. "Have *you* met my dad yet?"

"No. Sorry, I've got to get ready for my dance performance. Mom, Dad," Stephanie called to her parents, "it's time to head to the dance studio."

Andie started down the drive to meet her father. "Wait one more second," she called over her shoulder. She was so excited. As soon as she introduced her dad to everybody, she'd take him to see Magic. She'd groomed and polished him to perfection. He was definitely ready to show off.

"Mom!" Andie heard Mary Beth yell.

Andie stopped and turned to see what Mary Beth was shouting about. Her roommate was racing from the direction of the stables. Her face was bright red.

"Did—Tammy—come—back—here?" Mary Beth called, out of breath.

"No." Mrs. Finney's brows rose. "Why? Where is she?"

"I took her to the stable office to go to the bathroom," Mary Beth gasped when she reached the group. "I had to go, too, so I told her to wait outside until I was done. But when I came out, she was gone!"

Andie didn't know why Mary Beth was so worried. Tammy seemed like the kind of kid who'd wander off after butterflies.

"I bet she's just looking at the horses," Mr. Finney said. "You know how much she likes any kind of animal."

Mary Beth shook her head frantically. "No." Tears welled in her eyes. "She's not at the barn. She's not around the ring. I've checked *everywhere*. Tammy's really gone!"

10

"Oh, come on, Mary Beth," Andie said. "Your dad's right—Tammy's got to be somewhere close by."

Mr. Finney hugged his older daughter. "Don't worry, honey. We'll find her."

"I'll help you look," Lauren volunteered. She was still mounted on Whisper.

Mary Beth nodded, then sniffed. She didn't look very reassured.

"Well, *I've* got to get changed for my dance recital," Stephanie said impatiently. "Mom and Dad, are you coming? Lauren can untack Whistle by herself."

"It's *Whisper*," Lauren said.

Andie looked down the drive. Her father had almost reached the ring. "I'd help, too, but

I have to show my dad Magic before it gets too late." She was already dressed in her breeches and high, black boots.

"You girls run along," Mrs. Finney said, making shooing movements with her hands. "We can find Tammy ourselves. The campus isn't such a very big place, and with Tammy's red hair...Benji, you take Reed and go check again by the stable."

"Andie!" Mr. Perez called. He was puffing a bit from the climb. Excitedly, Andie ran the last few feet to greet him.

"I'm so glad you finally got here." Andie hesitated, unsure whether to hug him. Her dad reached over and squeezed her shoulders.

Andie looked up at her father. Then she looked back at the Remicks and Finneys. Mary Beth was biting her lip as if she were trying to keep from crying.

"I want you to meet Mary Beth's and Lauren's families," Andie said, her words tumbling out in a rush. She couldn't believe how nervous she was.

Andie led her father over to the group. "Glad to meet you," Mr. Perez said, shaking hands with everybody. Andie couldn't help noticing how tan and handsome he was. She was so proud of him.

"Sorry to rush off," Mr. Finney said to Mr. Perez. "But we seem to have lost a daughter."

"Oh?" Mr. Perez raised his brows in concern.

Mary Beth burst into tears. "I've been looking forward to this visit for weeks and now Tammy gets lost."

"Mary Beth's been pretty homesick," Lauren said, as if trying to explain Mary Beth's behavior. "She got a little overexcited about your coming for Parents' Weekend."

"It's all my fault," Mary Beth continued to sob.

"You'll find Tammy," Andie told her. She was impatient to leave. It was almost three o'clock. The family hoedown started at five. She wanted to have plenty of time to ride Magic for her dad.

Just then, Benji and Reed ran up.

"No sign of her," Benji said.

Mr. Finney frowned. "All right, gang, let's spread out. We'd better alert someone from the school."

"I'll go to the main office," Lauren said. "It's

in the administration building. I just have to take Whisper back to the stable."

"Can we help, too?" Mr. Perez asked.

No way, Andie almost protested. Then she realized what she was doing. Once again, she was thinking only about herself.

"Right," Andie said quickly. "My dad and I can check in the new barn. Okay, Mary Beth?"

Mary Beth grinned weakly. "Okay."

"This way, Dad." Andie started toward the barn where Jina kept Superstar. Side by side, she and her father walked in silence. Andie didn't have a clue what to say to him.

"So how's work?" she finally blurted out at the same moment he asked, "How's school?"

They both laughed nervously.

"School's okay." Andie glanced shyly at him. "I guess you know all about it, though."

He nodded. "Yes, Dean Wilkes has kept me well informed," he said with a chuckle.

"That's good." Andie wondered if he already knew about this morning's trash detail.

She stopped in front of the large, sliding barn door. It was already partly open. Jina and her mother were standing in the aisle where Superstar was crosstied. Ms. Golden was feeding the gray Thoroughbred an apple. Todd

Jenkins, Jina's trainer from Middlefield, was there, too. He was tall and cute with a slender build. Andie wondered if Lauren still had a crush on him.

Todd ran his hand down the front leg that Superstar had bowed a month ago. "Looks much better," he told Jina.

When Andie and her father came up to them, the introductions started all over again.

"You must be Myra Golden, the talk show host," Mr. Perez said.

Myra's amber eyes danced. "That's me. Do you like my show?"

"I've never seen it," Mr. Perez replied. "Not that I don't want to," he explained quickly. "I rarely watch TV unless it's the stock reports."

"Oo-ooh, I love those stock reports, too," Myra replied. "They're so exciting." She and Mr. Perez started to laugh.

Grown-ups, Andie thought, rolling her eyes.

"We're looking for Mary Beth's little sister," she told Jina. "Have you seen her?"

Jina shook her head. "No. I just finished riding Applejacks." She pointed down the aisle. Through the open door at the other end, Andie could see the front of a horse van. A high-pitched whinny burst from the van. "Todd brought him from Middlefield so my mom could meet him."

"How'd he do?" Andie asked.

Jina made a face. "He was awful."

"Not awful," Todd said, chuckling. He had unfastened the crossties and was leading Superstar to his stall.

"He almost bucked me off," Jina told him, frowning. Then she turned back to Andie. "Did you say Tammy was missing?"

Andie nodded. "Yeah. We're all looking for her."

"Oh, dear," Myra Golden said. "How old is the child?"

"About three, I guess," Andie said. "We don't think she's gone very far."

"We'll help you look," Jina offered. "Won't we, Mom?"

"Of course," Myra said. "Where shall we start?"

"How about the woods behind the paddock?" Andie suggested. "I'll check the barn."

Everyone began to spread out in different directions.

Andie headed down the aisle, peering into each stall. Most of them were empty, since the new barn was only used for horses owned by students.

Maybe I'll be keeping Magic in here soon, Andie couldn't help thinking.

"Tammy?" she called as she rounded the corner. She could hear Applejacks nickering again. He didn't sound very happy to be cooped up in the van.

Andie shook her head. Searching the barn was a waste of time, she decided. Tammy was probably in one of the dorms, mooching candy from some of the students.

She checked all of the stalls anyway. At the last one, a tall, white horse stuck his head over the bottom door. It was Snowman, who belonged to one of the senior girls. Andie didn't know him very well. She patted him on the neck and was about to turn back when a small, dark shape in the far corner of his stall caught her eye.

Andie pushed Snowman's head out of the way and peered closer. Her heart began to thump. The dark shape was wearing a navy jacket. Red hair peeked above the straw.

It was Tammy!

"Todd! Jina! Dad!" Andie shouted. Without thinking, she flung open the door and dashed into the stall. Snowman pinned his ears, startled by the intrusion. But Andie ignored him. She dropped to her knees next to Tammy.

The little girl was curled in a ball, her thumb stuck in her mouth. She was fast asleep. Andie almost cried with relief.

"Andie! What in the world—?" Todd reached the stall first. He came into the stall and grabbed Snowman by the halter. Jina, Myra, and Mr. Perez were right behind him.

"It's Tammy," Andie said. "Somebody go get the Finneys. I think she's okay."

"I'll go," Mr. Perez said.

Just then, Tammy's lids began to flutter. She looked up at Andie blankly.

"Who are you?" she finally asked in a bewildered voice.

Andie hugged her. "It's Andie. Remember me? Are you okay?"

"Yes." Tammy yawned and rubbed her eyes. Straw clung to her hair, and her cheeks were streaked with dirt as if she'd been crying. "I got lost."

"What were you doing in Snowman's stall?"

Tammy grinned up at the big horse. "Oh, he was bery nice. I took a nap with him."

"Are you sure you're okay, honey?" Myra asked the little girl. She crouched down beside Andie.

Tammy's eyes grew wide as saucers. "Wow! You're that lady on TV!"

"Tammy! Sweetie!" Just then, the whole Finney family rushed into the barn. Tammy put her arms around Andie's neck and hung on as Andie lifted her up and carried her into the aisle.

Mrs. Finney grabbed her little daughter and hugged her tight to her chest. "You scared us half to death!"

Mary Beth started crying again, and Benji, Reed, and Dogums ran around yelling and barking. Snowman tossed his head at all the noise.

"I just took a nap," Tammy said.

"In a horse's stall?" Mary Beth cried. "You could have been stomped—"

Andie clapped a hand over Mary Beth's mouth. "Shh!" she whispered. "You don't need to tell her that. She's fine."

Mary Beth's shoulders drooped in relief. "You're right. And thanks, Andie. You were great."

Andie bit back a grin as she looked over at Tammy. The little girl was chattering away about her adventure. It really did feel good to know that she was all right—and that she, Andie, had found her.

Then Andie glanced over at her father. He was smiling at her proudly.

Andie's heart felt as if it would burst with happiness.

"So what do you think of him, Dad?" Andie asked as she finished buckling Magic's girth.

Mr. Perez nodded slowly as he gazed at the Thoroughbred.

Andie waited for an answer, trying to be patient. But ever since she'd shown Magic to her dad, he hadn't said a word. He just leaned on the stall door, watching as she bridled and saddled him.

She couldn't stand it any longer.

"Well? *Well?*" she repeated.

Mr. Perez chuckled. "Relax, young lady. It's not like I know very much about horses."

"You don't have to," Andie said. "Just pretend he's a human athlete." She waved her hand at Magic's shoulder and hindquarters. "Look at the power in those muscles."

Magic threw up his head and snorted at her. "And look at that gleam of intelligence in his eyes. Look—"

"Okay, okay!" Mr. Perez held up his palms. "I give up. You've done a fine job with this animal. I'm proud of you."

Andie clapped her hands excitedly. "Thanks! Are you ready to watch me ride him?"

"I suppose so." Mr. Perez checked his watch. "Do we have time?"

"Yes!" Andie blurted out, even though she

knew they had only half an hour. "I wish we could miss that stupid hoedown," she grumbled. "It'll be just like all those other dumb Foxhall events."

"Now, Andie," her father warned in that tone she hated.

Andie opened the stall door and led Magic out. The earlier rush of activity at the stable was over, and things were pretty quiet.

That was good, Andie decided. She didn't need anything setting Magic off.

As she led the Thoroughbred toward the paddock behind the new barn, Andie did some deep breathing.

Relax, relax, she told herself. She rolled her shoulders, trying to loosen the knot between them. She'd waited weeks for this chance to show off Magic to her dad, and she didn't want to blow it.

When they rounded the corner of the barn, Andie's heart sank. Jina had turned Superstar out in the adjoining paddock.

Eager for company, Superstar lifted his head and whinnied loudly. He was wearing his bright blue blanket, the same one that had spooked Magic the other day.

Magic stopped dead. Head high, he whinnied back to Superstar. The gray pranced along the fenceline, shaking his head playfully.

This won't work, Andie thought. *Magic will get too excited.*

So what was she going to do? By the time she caught Superstar and put him in his stall, it would be too late to ride. And tomorrow, her father had to leave right after breakfast.

"What's wrong?" Mr. Perez asked.

"Nothing," Andie said quickly. Turning, she led Magic back toward the main barn. "I'll have to ride in the big ring."

You've never ridden Magic in the big ring before, a nagging voice reminded her.

So what? Andie answered right back. *I can do it. Magic can do it.*

Teeth clenched, she marched Magic past the main barn to the ring's gate. She hesitated before opening it.

The ring was huge. If Magic spooked, it would be tough to get him under control.

"Is everything okay?" her father asked as he came up behind her.

"Perfect." Andie smiled at her dad, pretending that everything was fine. Then she opened the gate and led Magic into the ring. The horse glanced around, curious but calm.

Andie checked her girth, then lowered one stirrup so she could mount without assistance. Her father leaned on the top rail to watch.

When she finally swung into the saddle, she took several breaths, then patted Magic reassuringly.

"We can do it," she whispered to him as she leaned over to shorten her stirrup.

Straightening, she squared her shoulders. She gathered the reins, then asked him to walk, making sure to use only a voice command. Magic walked down the side of the ring with long, rhythmic strides. Using light pressure on the reins, Andie kept him at one end. She did a figure eight, trotted several circles, and halted him in front of her father.

"Whew." Andie gave Magic's neck a hug. *We did it!* she told him silently. Then she grinned at her dad. "Wasn't that great? Could you see how light and responsive he was? And I've only been riding him for one week!"

"Yes, that was very nice," Mr. Perez said. But Andie could tell by the tone of his voice that he wasn't impressed. Not that she blamed him. Walking and trotting weren't very exciting to watch.

"He's going to be a great jumper," Andie added.

"Oh, really?" Mr. Perez checked his watch. "Look, Andie, we only have ten more minutes—"

Andie's stomach fluttered nervously.

Was her father bored? Or was it that he couldn't see what a great horse Magic was?

"Really, Dad. He's going to be a terrific jumper," Andie repeated. "Mrs. Caufield says he has great potential."

Andie told him how Magic loved it when she'd longed him over poles on the ground. "I bet he'll be able to jump four feet easily," she bragged.

Her father raised one brow.

"You don't believe me, do you?" Andie's fingers tightened on the reins.

She could see it in her father's eyes—the way he glanced toward the main buildings. Her father *was* bored. And if he wasn't impressed with Magic, he wouldn't buy him for her.

Panicking, Andie racked her brains for some way to convince her father how wonderful Magic was. Maybe it would help if she could prove he was a good jumper.

"Do you want to see him jump?" she asked quickly. "We'll jump that small cavalletti in the middle of the ring."

She pointed to a low pole held up by two X's at each end. It was only about three inches high. Nothing exciting, but it would show her father how well Magic could jump.

Mr. Perez frowned. "Well, are you sure—?"

"Just watch!" Andie cut him off. Turning Magic, she walked him toward the pole, halting him in front so he could see it.

Her heart was racing, her palms sweating, but she ignored them. She *had* to take this chance. She *had* to prove to her father that Magic was the right horse for her.

"Let's do it, guy," Andie told the Thoroughbred. She trotted him in a circle, then steered him down the middle of the ring.

As they approached the cavalletti, Magic's ears flicked back and forth. Then his pace quickened. Andie grabbed a hunk of mane high up his neck, preparing for a sudden hop.

You've jumped a zillion times before, she reassured herself. *This isn't any different.* Still, her heart pounded furiously.

A stride before the fence, Magic arched his

neck and leaped. Like an uncoiling spring, he shot into the air, throwing Andie backward. She hit the saddle with a hard *whap*.

Up, up, up. Magic seemed to soar forever before landing on the other side of the pole. Andie held tight to his mane, but her feet flew from the stirrups.

Pleased with his jump, Magic ducked his head and bucked playfully, throwing Andie out of the saddle. His mane ripped from her grasp, and she dove through the air, landing hard on her right side.

12

"Andie!" Mr. Perez cried out, jumping over the railing.

Coughing and gasping, Andie rolled onto her back. Then a stabbing pain in her right knee hit her, and she inhaled sharply.

She was hurt!

Tears welled in Andie's eyes. Already she could feel her knee swelling, the top of her tight boot pinching the flesh. But she didn't care.

I've really blown it this time.

Now her father would never buy Magic. And it was all her own fault.

"Honey, are you all right?" Her father rushed up and kneeled beside her.

She nodded. "Yes," she lied. "I just got the wind knocked out of me. Is Magic okay?"

Andie propped herself up on one arm. Magic was prancing around the ring, his reins dangling. The time he'd thrown Katherine Parks, the skittish horse had raced around the ring, terrified. But this time, Andie could tell he was just feeling good.

"Don't worry about the horse," her father said sharply. "Let's make sure *you're* all right."

"I'm fine," Andie repeated impatiently. What could she say to convince him that the accident wasn't Magic's fault? "Did you see how high Magic cleared that puny cavalletti?" she asked eagerly. "Didn't I tell you he could jump?"

Mr. Perez frowned. "Yes, you did. But you didn't tell me he would throw you off afterward!"

Andie ignored her father's angry tone. "He didn't throw me." She held out her hand. "Can you help me up? I need to catch Magic before he trips on his reins."

And before Dorothy or Mrs. Caufield see him running loose, she added to herself.

"Are you sure you should get up?" her father asked. Brow still furrowed, he studied her anxiously.

Andie nodded. "I'm sure." She sat up, trying not to wince.

Mr. Perez slipped his arm under his daughter's shoulders and lifted her. But when Andie put weight on her right leg, she cried out in pain.

"You're *not* okay," Mr. Perez said firmly. "Don't move, I'm getting help."

"No, Dad, I'm fine!" Andie grabbed onto the hem of his sweater, trying to keep him from leaving. "And Magic didn't throw me off. It was my fault."

But her father wasn't listening. He pulled away from her and, jogging from the ring, headed for the stable office.

Andie groaned and sank back into the tanbark. When Caufield saw her, it would be all over—for her and Magic.

"See, I told you I was okay," Andie said with false cheerfulness. She was sitting on the edge of the bed in the hospital examining room. Her dad was leaning tiredly against the wall. "The X rays prove it."

"Well, you're not exactly okay," said the young emergency room physician. He was wrapping her knee with an Ace bandage.

Andie gritted her teeth against the pain.

"You didn't break anything, but you do have a hematoma," the doctor continued.

"A hematoma?" Andie wrinkled her nose. Her knee had swelled to twice its usual size and was gradually turning black and blue. "What's that?"

"A bad bruise." The doctor secured the wrap and stood up. "So keep your leg elevated and an ice pack on your knee until the swelling goes down. And stay completely off that leg for at least twenty-four hours."

"But that's a whole day!" Andie protested. She squinted at the name tag on the doctor's white coat. DR. PREVIN. "Are you sure you know what you're talking about?" she asked doubtfully.

"Andie!" her father said sternly.

Dr. Previn smiled. "Yes, you are definitely going to have to stay off that leg."

"What about crutches?" Andie asked anxiously. "I can use crutches, right?"

The doctor shook his head. "Not until the swelling goes down. And no riding until there's absolutely no pain—that may be at least a week."

Andie groaned and slumped back on the

bed. A whole week until she could ride Magic again!

Then she stopped herself. She wasn't even sure she would be allowed to ride Magic again. When Caufield had rushed out to the ring with her dad, she hadn't said a word.

Neither had her father—the whole way to the hospital. He hadn't even spoken to her the whole time they'd sat in the waiting room.

"I'll send the nurse in with a wheelchair," Dr. Previn said.

"Oh, goody," Andie muttered when he'd left.

Her father turned to her. "You ought to be glad it's only your knee that's injured, young lady," he said, his voice tight. "You could have been killed. Whatever possessed you to try such a foolish stunt? I had no *idea* you had never jumped Magic before or I never would have allowed it."

"Okay, okay. It was a stupid thing to do," Andie said. "But we didn't have much time, and I had to do something special to show you how wonderful Magic is."

"Well, all you succeeded in was showing me how crazy that animal is!" Mr. Perez twirled his finger by his temple.

"He's not crazy!" Andie protested. "He just jumped higher than I expected."

"No—he—didn't," Mr. Perez said slowly, trying to keep his voice low and calm. "He bucked you off."

Andie opened her mouth to argue, but she knew her father was right. Magic *had* bucked her off, but she hadn't told Mrs. Caufield that. If the riding director ever found out the truth, Andie would never be allowed anywhere near Magic again.

Andie shook her head. "You're wrong. He didn't buck, he *jumped* me off," she lied. "And how would you know what a buck is, anyway? You were the one who said you didn't know anything about horses."

Mr. Perez turned away in frustration, just as the nurse came in pushing a wheelchair.

Andie glanced sideways at her father. His jaw was clenched angrily.

Her heart sank. She might as well face it— there was no way she was going to convince him that the accident wasn't Magic's fault.

Never in a million years.

"You broke your leg?" Lauren gasped an hour later. She, Mary Beth, and Jina were clustered

103

around Andie's bed in the school infirmary.

"No. I didn't break my leg," Andie explained for the third time. "I have a hematoma. That means a bad bruise."

"A bruise? Then why is your knee so big?" Jina asked, frowning.

Andie sighed. She was stretched out in the bed, still wearing her dirty breeches. Her right lower leg was propped on two pillows and an ice pack was draped over her knee.

Earlier, Mrs. Zelinski, the school nurse, and her father had helped her upstairs to the infirmary. Then her father had left.

"My knee is big because it swelled up," Andie explained. "Mrs. Caufield could barely get the boot off. And now there's an Ace bandage wrapped around it." She lifted the ice pack to show her roommates her knee. The doctor had cut up her breeches to her thigh.

"Boy, Mrs. Caufield must have been furious," Mary Beth said solemnly.

Andie ignored her.

"So tell us again what happened," Jina said. She'd just gotten back from eating out at a restaurant with her mom. Lauren and Mary

Beth had arrived soon after the hoedown was over.

Andie sighed, then launched into her version of the story—the one where Magic had jumped so high, she'd lost her balance and fallen off.

"At least you know he can jump," Lauren said.

"Try and explain that to my father," Andie grumbled. "He thinks Magic is some wild mustang or something."

Mary Beth raised her brows. "Well, he *is* pretty unpredictable."

"Oh, shut up," Andie muttered. She didn't want to hear any more bad things about Magic. "So how was the hoedown?" she asked, trying to change the subject.

"Oh, it was lots of fun!" Lauren said. "We square-danced and ate fried chicken and bobbed for apples."

"And how's Tammy?" Andie asked Mary Beth.

"Great, until she ate three pieces of cherry pie. Then she threw up on some corn stalks."

Andie had to laugh. It was the funniest thing she'd heard all night.

"All right, girls!" Mrs. Zelinski bustled around the curtain, clapping her hands. "Visiting time is over. Andie needs to get a sponge bath and go to sleep."

"A sponge bath!" Andie sat straight up. "No way!"

Jina, Lauren, and Mary Beth began to laugh hysterically.

"So long, Andie." Lauren wiggled her fingers as the three of them left. "Enjoy that sponge bath."

"Wait! Guys! Don't leave me!" Andie called. She could hear them still giggling as they went down the hall.

Slumping back against the pillow, she peered suspiciously at Mrs. Zelinski. The nurse was humming as she sloshed a washcloth in a soapy basin. Mustache hairs darkened her upper lip.

Had old Zelinski always looked like a gorilla? Andie wondered.

"Now then," the nurse said cheerfully. She turned, and Andie saw the gleam of scissors in her hand. "Let's get those dirty old pants off."

13

Breakfast in bed is supposed to be fun, Andie thought as another forkful of scrambled eggs dropped onto the blanket, *not messy like this.*

She gave up on the eggs and reached for a piece of toast. When she bit into it, crumbs sprinkled down the front of her nightie. She brushed them off, smearing butter on the sheet.

Andie hunted for her napkin, only to find it had fallen on the floor. And when she reached for the milk that Mrs. Zelinski had set on the bedside table, her arm wasn't quite long enough.

"Hi, Andie." Jina and Lauren came around the partition, grinning cheerfully.

"How's your knee?" Lauren asked.

"Good." Andie grinned back. She'd never

been so happy to see anybody in her life. "It's breakfast that's giving me big trouble. Can one of you get my milk and napkin?"

"Sure." Jina picked the napkin off the floor.

Andie tilted her head back. "Stick it under my chin," she instructed, "like a bib."

"There." Jina smoothed the napkin onto Andie's chest. Lauren handed her the glass of milk. Andie drank greedily, then started on her toast.

"Did you guys have a nice time with your parents?" she asked between chews.

"Great," Lauren said. She sighed. "I didn't want them to leave this morning."

Jina sat on the edge of the bed. "I had a good time, too. It's the first chance my mom and I have had to have dinner together since—"

"Can one of you get my brush?" Andie interrupted, pointing to her backpack on a chair. Her roommates had brought it over last night, packed with a few things. Her father was coming to say good-bye, and she wanted to look as if nothing had happened. She was determined to change his mind about Magic.

"Sure." Jina rummaged through the backpack and pulled out the hairbrush. She passed it to Andie. "So my mom and I got to talk about some—"

"Maybe you'd better move the tray before I spill everything," Andie suggested.

"Okay." Lauren picked up the tray and looked around the room, trying to decide where to put it.

Andie waved toward Mrs. Zelinski's desk. "Just set it there. It's not like the old gorilla does anything important. Can you imagine she wanted to *cut* off my breeches last night? I told her they cost almost a hundred bucks and if she touched them she was dead. The doctor already messed them up enough."

Lauren looked shocked. "You did *not* tell her that."

Andie grinned mischievously. "Well, she didn't cut them. I made her pull them off." She grimaced. "It hurt like crazy, too."

"When are you going to be able to walk on your leg?" Jina asked.

"Oh, soon," Andie said. "So did all the Finneys leave yet?" she asked, changing the subject.

Lauren shook her head. "They're still eating breakfast. Mary Beth's already crying. Every time one of her brothers or her sister says something, she hugs them and says how much she'll miss them."

"Those brats?" Andie snorted. "I'd be glad to see them go. Just like I'll be glad to see my father go."

"You won't be glad to see him go," Jina said.

"I will," Andie declared stubbornly. "He hates Magic. I know he won't buy him when the semester is up. And if he doesn't, I'll hate him for the rest of his life!"

Crossing her arms in front of her chest, Andie slumped back against the pillow. Out of the corner of her eye, she saw Jina and Lauren exchange glances.

"What are you two looking at?" she muttered.

Jina shrugged. Lauren bit a fingernail.

"You think Magic's crazy, too. Just like everybody else."

Jina shook her head. "No one thinks he's crazy. Just high-strung. Making him jump yesterday was dumb. As usual, you were just doing what *you* wanted," she added.

"Right," Lauren chimed in boldly. "We heard you were showing off for your dad— that's why you got in trouble."

"I wasn't showing off." Andie glared at Jina,

then at Lauren. Tears filled her eyes.

"Then why did you jump him?" Jina asked.

Andie shook her head. Why bother telling them? Her roommates wouldn't understand. No one would. Everyone thought she was just a reckless show-off.

"Andie," Lauren said, quietly this time, "you love Magic. We know you wouldn't do anything to hurt him."

Andie looked down at her hands. A tear fell on the sheet.

"Maybe if you can explain what happened to us first," Jina continued, "you'll be able to explain it better to your dad and Mrs. Caufield."

Slowly, Andie nodded. "Okay." She took a deep breath. "By the time we found Tammy, I didn't have much time to ride Magic. And when I did ride him, I could tell my dad wasn't real thrilled. I mean, he doesn't like horses anyway, and all Magic and I did was walk and trot. So I thought maybe if I showed him that Magic could jump, he'd see that he really *is* a special horse."

Jina and Lauren looked at each other again.

"Well, that makes more sense," Lauren said.

Just then someone knocked on the door.

Jina stood up and peeked around the partition.

"It's your father," she whispered.

Quickly, Andie tore the napkin from under her chin and flipped her hair behind her shoulders.

"We'd better go." Lauren gave Andie a thumbs-up, and she and Jina left.

"Andie?" Mr. Perez peered hesitantly around the curtain.

"Hi." Andie sat a little straighter. Her father came in, stopping at the foot of the bed. His hands were shoved in his pants pockets, and she saw that he had shadows under his eyes.

"How are you feeling this morning?" he asked, glancing everywhere but at her.

"I'm fine," Andie said. "I think the swelling's down already. And Mrs. Zelinski says she has crutches, so it won't be long before I'm on my feet. You heard the doctor—I'll be riding Magic again in a week."

There, she'd said it. Andie caught her breath, wondering how her father would respond.

"Well." Her father cleared his throat and put on his best businessman's expression—the one that showed no emotion. "I spoke with Mrs. Caufield last night."

Andie groaned silently. That didn't sound good.

"She thinks Magic is a special horse, too. She says all riders take risks every time they mount."

Andie's eyes widened. Was Caufield actually on her side?

"She did admit that you take more risks than most of her students." He frowned down at the floor. "But she also thinks you learned your lesson this time. And because an adult was with you, and you had permission to ride Magic, you didn't really break any rules."

Caufield said that? Andie couldn't believe it.

"She did agree that what you did was foolish." Mr. Perez paused and looked at Andie, his eyes steely. "She also agrees that Magic might not be the best horse for you."

"What?" Andie's jaw dropped. She should have known all the grown-ups would be against her. "But that's not fair. I love Magic. No one seems to see that he *is* the right horse for me." Angrily, she twisted her body on the bed, trying to get away from her father.

Mr. Perez stepped closer. His voice softened. "Andie, I know you love that horse. And it hurts me to do this, but—" He hesitated.

Andie squeezed her eyes tight and buried her head in the pillow. She didn't want to sob in front of her father.

"When I saw you lying there yesterday, hurt, it made me realize how much I love you." Mr. Perez faltered, then went on. "And I realized, too, that I couldn't buy an animal that might hurt you again. It's too much of a risk."

Reaching down, he touched her hand. "I hope you understand," he whispered. "I'll give you a call soon." Then he strode from the room.

When she was sure her father was gone, Andie burst into tears. Magic wasn't going to be hers. Ever.

But that wasn't the only reason she was crying.

Her father had said he loved her.

For the first time that she could remember.

14

Andie woke with a start. Her head was pounding.

Had she been having a nightmare?

No, her father *had* been here.

And he'd told her that he'd never buy Magic.

Sadness washed over her. She sank back into the pillow and pulled the covers over her head.

Parents' Weekend had been a total disaster.

Everything that she'd worried about had come true.

Then Andie flipped the covers off her head. She'd almost forgotten. It hadn't been a total disaster.

Her father had said he loved her. And maybe he'd change his mind about Magic someday.

Andie felt a rush of happiness. She had to go see Magic! On Sundays she always brushed him and gave him a treat.

Throwing back the sheet, she swung her legs to the side of the bed. The ice pack fell to the floor. Her knee was already beginning to throb.

Andie struggled to her feet. Hopping on her left leg, she reached for her dirty sweatshirt and breeches hanging over the back of the chair. She sat in the chair and pulled the sweatshirt over her nightie. Gritting her teeth, she slowly pulled on the breeches. Even though one leg had been cut, she had to tug them hard over her fat knee and the pain made her head swim.

But she had to do it. She had to see Magic. She had to see Mrs. Caufield and explain what happened. Jina and Lauren had understood. Maybe the riding director would understand, too.

When her breeches were zipped, Andie hunted around for shoes. Her father had taken her riding boots back to the suite. Not that they would have fit around her swollen leg. So what was she going to wear?

Turning, she rummaged in her backpack. Her roommates had tucked in a pair of moccasins. She slipped them on and silently thanked Jina and Lauren.

Andie hopped over to the infirmary window and looked out. The sky was heavy with gray clouds. Bare tree limbs whipped back and forth. She'd freeze before she ever reached the stable.

"And what are you doing out of bed, young lady?" a stern voice asked.

Mrs. Zelinski was standing by the partition, her hands on her hips.

"Nothing," Andie said innocently.

"Nothing?" The nurse raised a dark brow. "Then why are you dressed in those dirty clothes?"

"Um." Andie looked down. "I was cold." Then she grinned guiltily. "Actually, I *was* trying to sneak out—before my father left Foxhall. I need to give him a message."

"Oh?" Mrs. Zelinski didn't look convinced.

Andie nodded. "Really. Do you have a piece of paper? I could write it down and you could give it to him."

Mrs. Zelinski cocked her head. "Now that makes more sense. You get back in bed and put that ice pack on your knee."

Andie hopped obediently into bed. Mrs. Zelinski came back with a pad and pencil.

I love you, too, Andie wrote carefully. Folding it, she handed it to the nurse. "Please make sure he gets it. His car's parked in the lot by Bracken Hall."

"I'll make sure," Mrs. Zelinski said, patting her shoulder. "You just rest that leg."

Andie smiled sweetly. The instant Mrs. Zelinski was out the door, she jumped from bed and hobbled over to the closet where the nurse kept the crutches.

She stuck them under her armpits. They were a perfect fit. She hopped out the door and down the hall, her right calf swinging in the air. When she reached the steps, she threw down the crutches. They thumped noisily to the landing.

Holding on to the rail, Andie managed to reach the first floor. Since it was Sunday, the main hall of Old House was quiet. Still, she could hear voices from one of the offices.

Andie's heart beat wildly. If she could just

make it out the back door before Zelinski returned or someone else saw her, she'd be home free.

She picked up her crutches and moved awkwardly down the hall as fast as she could. But when she reached the heavy exit door, she stopped dead. Footsteps were coming down the hall.

She'd never get it open in time!

"Andie? Is that you?" someone called.

Andie twirled around, almost falling off her crutches. Lauren, Jina, and Mary Beth were hurrying down the hall.

"Of course it's me," Andie snapped, trying to calm the butterflies in her stomach. "Who else would be skulking around on crutches?"

"You don't have to be so nasty," Lauren said. "We didn't mean to scare you."

"What are you doing?" Mary Beth asked.

"Trying to break out of this place." Andie brightened. "Hey! Will one of you open the door for me?"

"But where are you going?" Jina persisted. "You're not supposed to be walking on that leg."

"I'm not." Andie realized this was getting

her nowhere. Zelinski would be here any second. "Look, guys, I need your help—fast. I've got to get to the stables and talk to Caufield—before she does something dumb like getting rid of Magic or assigning me to another horse."

Lauren shook her head. "I don't know if we should help you, Andie. It seems like you only get in more trouble."

"True," Andie agreed quickly. "And after this, I promise—no more trouble."

"Sure," Mary Beth and Jina chorused. They didn't look at all convinced.

Andie sighed. Her shoulders sagged, and her knee was killing her. She couldn't really blame her roommates for acting this way. Lauren was right. She was always getting into trouble.

"I'm sorry." Andie said finally. "You three have been the best. Thanks for all you've done…" Her voice trailed off.

Her roommates grinned at each other.

"That's all we needed to hear," Lauren said as she pushed open the exit door.

"Huh?" Andie said, puzzled.

"An apology," Mary Beth explained as she

took Andie's upper arm. "You *have* been a pain."

"Definitely," Jina agreed heartily as she and Mary Beth helped her out the door.

"But we do understand," Lauren said.

"You do?" Andie repeated, glancing back and forth at them.

Her friends nodded.

"We know how important Magic is to you," Jina explained. "And how upset you've been."

"So what are you going to do," Mary Beth asked, "now that your dad probably won't buy Magic?"

Andie shook her head. "I don't know. But I'll think of something."

"I believe *that*," Lauren said, and the girls all burst out laughing.

"We'd better hurry and get you up to the barn," Jina said, glancing down the hall, "before Mrs. Zelinski catches us busting you out of here."

"I'm ready." Andie secured the crutches under her arms, then glanced up the hill toward the stables. They seemed a million miles away.

She took a deep breath. Suddenly, her knee didn't hurt quite so much.

It wouldn't be easy, but with her roommates' help, Andie knew she would figure out what to do about Magic. Right now, all she needed to do was make it to the stables. She had a lot to tell Mrs. Caufield.

And Magic was waiting.

**Don't miss the next book
in the Riding Academy series:
#7: JINA'S PAIN-IN-THE-NECK
PONY**

"Jina, you've just *got* to let Mary Beth and me go with you to Middlefield Stables this afternoon," Lauren pleaded.

"Oh, come on, guys," Jina said. "Andie's not *that* bad."

"Oh, yes she is," Lauren declared. "And with no riding today, we'll be cooped up in the suite with her all afternoon and night." Desperately, she squeezed Jina's wrist. "She'll drive us crazy!"

"Besides," Mary Beth added, "we're dying to see you ride Applejacks. He's *so-o-o* cute and sweet."

Cute and sweet! Jina groaned silently. If only her roommates knew the truth.

That "cute, sweet" pony was a total brat!

ALISON HART has been horse-crazy since she was five years old. Her first pony was a pinto named Ted.

"I rode Ted bareback because we didn't have a saddle small enough," she says.

Now Ms. Hart lives and writes in Mt. Sidney, Virginia, with her husband, two kids, two dogs, one cat, her horse, April, and another pinto pony named Marble. A former teacher, she spends much of her time visiting schools to talk to her many Riding Academy fans. And you guessed it—she's still horse-crazy!

If you enjoy books about animals,
you'll love these wonderful classic stories
about a horse and his boy:

THE BLACK STALLION
THE BLACK STALLION RETURNS
SON OF THE BLACK STALLION
THE BLACK STALLION AND SATAN
THE BLACK STALLION'S BLOOD BAY COLT
THE BLACK STALLION'S COURAGE
THE BLACK STALLION MYSTERY
THE BLACK STALLION AND FLAME
THE BLACK STALLION AND THE GIRL
THE BLACK STALLION LEGEND
THE YOUNG BLACK STALLION